ONE KISS

CJ WARRANT

Paperback edition / ISBN #978-1-7332367-2-0

Ebook edition / ISBN #978-1-7332367-3-7

Cover Art by Anne Berkeley

Editing by Michelle Edrington-Areaux

"There is no love without forgiveness, and there is no forgiveness without love."
~Bryant H. McGill

CONTENTS

ONE KISS

ONE

TIM

"How can you be bored, Tim? You start your job at Children's in two weeks, and you are finally settled living here in San Antonio. With me! What more do you need?" My best friend, Freda Sanchez, let's go of my arm and heads to the fridge. "Take it easy and enjoy this mini vacation. I'm sure when work starts, you'll have a different tune." Freda fills her lunch bag with a bag of chips and a sandwich she made last night.

"You know I can't sit still. Besides, working at the hospital isn't going to stop me from looking to do things on the weekends, or on my days off," I admit with a bit of a lie. I can lounge in a pool like nobody's business. Yet, I worry my lower lip with my teeth as the truth to why I still feel unsettled.

It has been a month since I abruptly quit my nursing job at Shriners Hospital and moved from Los Angeles to San Antonio, Texas—thanks to Freda—who is willing to put me up in her second bedroom. The townhouse is small, but not too much that we don't' bounce off each other. I'm just grateful that I'm away from my ex who I caught graciously fucking a friend of mine in our bed. Hell, if I hadn't forgotten my ID badge that day, I wouldn't have caught them naked and already doing it like rabid bunnies in my four-poster bed. I would have gone along in my blissful ignorance.

Yeah. I shake the burned image out of my head while swallowing down the bitterness I'm drowning in. But that part of my life is over, and Justin is out of my life. I need to get over that asshole's betrayal and move on.

Except, how can I when my volatile feelings for Justin and Matthew's betrayal are sticking with me like painful burrs? No matter what I do, I can't shake off the anger and resentment. And let's not forget the embarrassment of not knowing they've been together for almost six months.

He's not worthy of you, I repeatedly tell myself—or try to believe it anyway. Then why do I keep replaying the words he spat at me that day?

"You're not the same, Tim. You've become a little old man. You're too afraid of your own

shadow to have any fun. Even the sex is boring."

That was a hard proverbial pill to swallow. Justin's echoed words spur something in me, and I look at Freda with more determination than before. "Maybe I should volunteer with you. If they take me right away." I grab the San Antonio Humane Society volunteer pamphlet off the counter and skim through it. "This is perfect for me. I can do it on my days off."

"You're scared of animals, honey. How are you going to volunteer when you can't be near an animal without running the opposite way?" Freda's thick black eyebrows are drawn tight as her dark brown eyes center on me. When this five-foot-five woman is focused you, she means business.

"Hey, I love animals—just not cats. For some reason they don't like me." I can't hide the embarrassment flooding my cheeks. "You know the history with me and cats."

"Tim." The annoyance in my name makes me wince. "I know."

I drop the pamphlet and shake my head. "Maybe you're right. I just can't sit…"

"Or, I'm wrong," Freda plasters on a small but affectionate smile. "Let me talk to Gina. She might have a job that has minimal contact with cats. Then maybe it will get you out of whatever funk you're in."

"Okay," I say with some relief. "Anything is better than being stuck here and looking at these four walls."

Feigned agitation creases her thick eyebrows. "Hey, my colorful walls are nice to look at."

"Yes, they are, and you're going to be late." I glance at the newly added wall clock in the kitchen.

"Oh crap, I'm going to be late. Sounds good, I'll call you later—and Tim?"

"Yes?" I turn and plaster on a smile that only skims the surface of what I'm really feeling.

"If you're serious about volunteering, then go to their website, SAhumane.org and register." She slips on her simple black heels and slings the bag over her shoulder.

"All right. Now get going or you'll be fired." I wave her off.

As a secretary for a large law firm near downtown, Freda's travel time is no less than twenty minutes, unless she stops at her local Starbucks, which I have a feeling she will today.

After Freda quickly brushes her long black hair up into a tight ponytail, she swipes several loose hairs off her green blouse and black pants. She checks her lipstick in the entry way mirror and calls out, "Text you," before shutting the door on our conversation.

"Sure." I refill my coffee mug and plant my ass on the stool. As I stare down at the pamphlet, the image on the front shows a volunteer holding a small white kitten gives me the willies.

I let out a large huff of breath. Freda's right. Maybe I should enjoy my time off before I start work. But studying the pamphlet, a memory from my grandparents' house and the mean old tabby named Tammy that used to terrorize me as a child jumps out of the dark recesses of my head.

Every time we visited their house, Tammy would meow and hiss at me until my grand-mother had to put her in one of the bedrooms. But one day, I must have gotten too close, because that little bitch scratched me right on my cheek. To this day, I have a small scar reminding me to keep away from any furry beasts.

The longer I sit in silence alone, the more determined I am to put myself out of my comfort zone. *Old man, ha.* I'll show you who's not an old man.

I won't let my fears control my life. I'm twenty-fucking-four, damn it. In order to move forward with my life, I need to face those challenges head on and not be afraid. Too bad, it's easier said than done.

TWO
TIM

After changing my mind several times, I finally signed up to volunteer. Freda was good on her word and talked to one of the supervisors and fast tracked me right away. They also promised to put me with duties away from the cats. Though, I don't know what those duties are.

"I'm nervous," I say, with some trepidation as Freda and I step into the main Humane Society red brick building on Fredericksburg Road, the following Saturday morning.

My legs are like cooked spaghetti, but I hope my nerves settle and enjoy the experience as I look around the large space. Front and center is the reception half circle desk where adoptees and adopters are greeted. Behind that, are two doors. There are both closed but I have a feeling the real action happens there.

"You'll be okay. Just listen to the lead and have fun with it," My best friend says, smiling. "Just keep an open mind, okay?"

"What do you mean?" I eye her with obvious puzzlement. Freda had been acting strange all morning, constantly reassuring me, but she was tight lipped and hasn't revealed a thing. Oh God, did they put me in the feline section? Is this some sort of therapy? I hope not.

Before she can answer, Freda is called away by one of the staff members.

I'm standing alone with the other new volunteers milling about the space. I stare down at my new purple shirt and proudly run my hands down the front. I hope Freda is right and my job will be handling more the dog side of the shelter.

A surge of excitement courses through me as a booming male voice calls through-out the room. "Can I have all the new volunteers follow me."

My head shoots up and I watch the ten or so people fall in line and enter a room down one hallway on the other side of the reception area. I'm at the end of the line, but follow along until I reach the staff lead with a blue shirt and clipboard.

His head is down, hence my reaction to the man takes a second too late for me to turn around and run. The moment I lock eyes on his face, my heart seizes to beat and I draw in a sharp breath before my mouth drops wide open. I stand there frozen before the one man I thought I'd never see again.

No way. No fucking way. James Cannon. Nothing changed. Same blond hair, same mesmerizing whiskey-colored eyes—and not to mention the blue shirt he's wearing that emphasizing his broad shoulders. The same broad shoulders I was enamored with in high school.

For some crazy reason, while my feet are cemented to the floor, my brain is going through an epileptic seizure, and my body won't respond and walk away.

The man I lusted after in high school is standing right in front of me. The same man who happened to be my tormentor. My bully for three of my four years in high school.

For some inconceivable reason, fate has it in for me and wants to screw with my life even more. Why not? Kick me while I'm down and let my self-confidence twist in pain. Punch me where I can't breathe, while my heart is hammering out of my chest and is about to explode from my ribs.

"Your name?"

Is he kidding?

How does he not know who I am? What, did he zap the three years he spent bullying me out of his mind? Grrr.

For some strange reason, his name spills from my lips before I clamp my mouth shut. "James Cannon."

"That's me." He smiles sweetly, but I don't buy what he's selling in those attractive dimpled cheeks, and the sparkle in his beautiful golden amber eyes.

Does he seriously think I would forget all the shit he did to me? Pushing me against the lockers. Taunting me in the locker room. Throwing food at me during lunch—and let's not forget all the homophobic garbage that came out of his mouth. No. I damn well know my appearance hasn't changed much, for him not to recognize me right away.

I'm still me. Short spike blond hair, light blue eyes—and all of five-feet-eight in height. Granted, I packed on a pound or two from the hospital cafeteria food during my clinicals—not to mention cardio time at the gym. But that was months ago. Now, I hardly work out, except for running. It's my way of coping and relieving stress, and I'm good at it.

James stares at me with such intensity, I realize we've been standing there for way too long than I intended. But with the look on his face, maybe I'm wrong on my assumption, and he doesn't know who I am.

For a brief second, relief centers me and my stomach doesn't want to jump up to my throat.

Then his eyes widen, a spark of recognition dawns in them. His gorgeous smile spreads, showing his white teeth like a great white shark and leans in close like he wants to take a bite. "You're Timothy Andrew Henry Scott."

"Don't call me that," I lash out without thought, a little too loudly while ignoring the shiver from his predatory grin.

My anger notches up from the way James is staring down at me with that familiar gleam in his eyes. That same look I once thought looked sexy, is now making my back molars grind to dust. To be honest, I'm not sure if I'm angrier at seeing James, or for him using my full name out loud.

Whenever my mother uses my full name, it's a scold. But out of that man's mouth, I want to maim.

I never understood why my parents gave me two middle names. So-what if each of my parents wants to pass on their fathers' names. Pick one and move on. But no, my parents had to be different.

However, in this moment, it doesn't matter if I have two middle names—or four first names—I don't give a shit if I have five. I'm not letting this dickhead get to me in any way, shape, or form. I'd be damned if I'm going to stand here and take what's he's shovelling. I had enough of James Cannon's bullshit to last me a lifetime. No more.

"My name is Tim Scott. Let's keep it that way." I stand tall, looking James right in the eyes. It doesn't matter if my stomach does a belly whoosh the moment our gazes meet.

"Hmm. All right, Tim Scott. It's nice to see you again." His cool demeanor is simply irritating me.

Did I just see him scoping out my body? No way.

"Not long enough," I say under my breath, averting my eyes while trying to remain somewhat calm, especially under the scrutiny of the staff. But it's hard to keep a level head where James Cannon is concerned. Now, I'm not sure volunteering is worth dealing with this jerk-face. I'm about to tell this asshole to shove the job and walk out. I straighten my spine a bit more and stare straight into his eyes, when a look on his face morphs into one I can't decipher.

"Yes. It's very nice to see you again, Tim." The sincerity and easy cadence in his words puts a heavy wedge of doubt in my confidence.

What was I thinking? This was definitely a bad idea coming here.

I'm about to say so when he interrupts me. "Sorry, Tim, but I'm on a timeline. I need to start the intro." The bastard shocks me by nudging me forward into the room and closing the door. I turn to chew him out for getting in my space, when every volunteer in a seat is staring at us like we're the main attraction at a circus.

Clamping my mouth shut to avoid any unnecessary attention, I take a seat at the back row. I fold my arms across my chest and glare daggers at James as he walks to the front of the room and starts casually talking about the duties of us volunteers. As several minutes pass, my arms gradually drop from my chest, and I put my listening ears on.

If I must stay, I might as well learn something about the job I come to do. Besides, I'm here for one reason; to volunteer. I'm not here for James or any other jerk. And if I can help it, I won't let him drive me away, either. I had one dickhole do that to me. I'm not going let this one get in my head any further than what he already marred.

I slip on my professional nurse's face and take in what the different jobs entail.

After thirty minutes of blah-blah blah, James finally asks, "Does anyone have any questions?"

An Asian girl, who looks no older than eighteen, raises her hand.

"Yes?" James replies sweetly, with a questioning smile. From my vantage point, I'm slightly taken aback on how approachable he looks and his attentiveness to answer the girl's question. So much so, that I don't pay attention to what she asked. My eyes fix on James and then his mouth. And his shoulders—

Grrr! Stop staring at the man as though he's on the menu.

I hate to admit it, but he's even more beautiful than he was in high school. Broader chest, thick ropy arms, short clipped blondish hair, and two-day old scruff on his face. James has a face of an angel. Granted, I know firsthand how this angel is really the devil in disguise. But I still can't help admiring him from afar.

James's attention quickly latches onto me, and my stomach flips in reaction. Did he catch me checking him out? Shit, I hope not. I can easily turn away and pretend to look at something else, but why? I won't let him intimidate me.

I pierce him with one of my death glares, which normally gets a reaction from people, but apparently James doesn't get the hint.

"Each of you will be partnering up to do the job you are assigned. And since we're one-person short today, I think… Tim, do you mind if we partner up together?"

My mouth can't drop open any wider.

One of his dark blond eyebrows rises high.

Damn it, he's challenging me.

I will not let this man get to me, I keep

telling myself, and quickly snap my composure together and think before I answer. I can be a total dick and decline to partner up with him because from what I'm seeing around the room, there are several women giving him googly eyes who would love to work with the douche-canoe.

Although, I'm in the mood to annoy the man. "Sure. Why not." The cheeriness in my voice is so fake, that the volunteers are looking at me strangely.

"Great. I put up a list on the back wall with all who are paired up and the jobs you'll be handling today. Have fun, be safe, and if you have questions, don't hesitate to ask anyone in a blue shirt."

I stay in my seat while the rest of the volunteers head to the wall. I studiously stare at James as he talks to an older woman, who has a taloned hand on his forearm, but his eyes are trained on me.

Then James's words finally hit me like a hammer to my brain. The list of volunteers was already tacked on the back wall. So that means that he already knew who the new incoming volunteers were, in order to make up the partner list. That bastard feigned knowing me in the beginning and now...

I'm too stunned to talk.

This whole time, James knew I was a part of this group. My shock shifts into humiliation. Without thinking, I jump up from my seat and storm out of the room without paying any mind to anyone around me. My feet move fast, and I find myself outside in the parking lot, heaving breaths as I try to control my racing heart.

The hell with this shit, I'm going home. I didn't come here to be a verbal whipping boy or a play-toy for James Cannon again.

I barely make it to my car, when a beefy hand grabs my forearm and stops me in my escape.

I don't have to turn to know it's James who has me in his hold and spins me around. "Take your hands off me, you bastard," I shout.

His hands are gone in an instant, but his face is inches from mine. "Lower your voice, Tim. I'm not here to hurt you."

I take a quick step back to get out of his space and get into my fighting stance. "I took defence classes, asshole. I'm no longer that pushover you bullied in high school."

James, who is well over six-feet some-thing, straightens into his full height and starts chuckling. Actually chuckling!

"What's so damn funny? You don't think I'm going to kick your ass?" I try to keep the tension in my voice and my fists in front of me. "You know what they say; the bigger you are, the harder you'll fall. And I'm about to show you how hard I can be on you."

"Umm." Another set of unrestrained laughter flies out of his mouth and tears seep out from the corners of his eyes.

"What's so damn funny?" I repeat, as I go over what I just said to him and immediately see the errors of my words. "Damn it," I groan out, throwing my hands up in defeat. I can't believe I set myself up like that.

"As much as I like to know how hard you might be on me, I'm not going to fight you, Tim." James leans against a dark grey Jeep as though he owns the vehicle and smiles down at me. "I told Freda that you're weren't over the high school thing—"

"Thing," I bark out. "You bullied me for three years, Cannon. Why would Freda think —Wait—Freda? Freda knew you worked here?" I narrow my eyes at James while contemplating murder of my best friend. "Damn it. I knew something was up."

Then the past week all comes together. Freda bringing up high school stuff. Even mentioning James a few times. Why didn't I see this coming?

"Yes. Who do you think brought her into the fold?"

"I should have known." I groan with irritation.

"Don't be mad at Freda—"

"I'll deal with Freda later, but you and I are done here." I push the finality of my words and turn to go.

"Tim, wait. I—I want to apologize—for everything." James's word strikes me still.

I turn back to him, and stark emotion shines in his eyes. I don't know how to react to the rawness of his words or that apologetic look on his face.

I take a single step toward him, jaw tight and a lump in my throat at what I'm about to say. "Okay. I'm listening." I don't care if I sound like a brat. This man owes me an apology—many apologies—and I want them now.

"I'm sorry. Truly. Who I was back then, and what I did and said to you was inexcusable. But that's not me anymore. I'm a different man—a better man—if you only look at me. I want to be friends and get to know you." James closes the gap between us. "Please."

I don't move, but I put a hand out to stop him from getting closer. "I'm a different man too, and I can spot a line of bullshit a mile away. But right now, I can't tell if you feeding me a line I want hear or you're being sincere. And being friends—"

"What's going on here?" A guy with blue shirt strides up and cuts me off. He stands almost even with James. The nametag on his shirt reads Grant. His deep frown is imbedded into his acne-scarred face. His light brown eyes darts from me to James with disgust. "I didn't know you moved the new volunteers meeting into the parking lot, Cannon. This isn't the time for dicking around with twirks. Keep your personal life out of the shelter."

Twirks? I don't get it.

"It's not like that, Grant, and you're telling me something I already know," James grates out, with a biting snap. "Now, if you'll excuse us."

"If this guy is giving you trouble, I'm here to help," Grant says with a hint of venom in his words, which the comment seems to be directed toward me. "We take things very seriously around here. We do things by the book. If you're not willing to follow the rules, then maybe it's best that your kind shouldn't be here."

"My kind?" I say with contempt. "What are you trying to suggest?"

"That's enough," James bites out at the same time.

"You know exactly what I'm suggesting, newbie." Grant points to me. At first, I thought he was warning me about James, then Grant's verbal diarrhea hit a nerve.

James steps in my line of sight, blocking Grant as though he's protecting me from the shitbag. I'm not sure how I feel about that. A bully protecting me from a bully.

"That is totally uncalled for. Wait until Trish hears about this." James's voice is even, but his words pack a punch. His stiff posture and shoulder muscles are rigid like steel girders as he leans, face to face with this Grant. I have a sudden urge to reach out to touch those ridges and dips of his back, but I restrain myself.

"Whatever." Grant glares at me and then stalks away.

"Don't mind him. Grant's harmless."

"Are you sure about that? I swear, he just showed me his sharp homophobic teeth." I glance over to where Grant rushed off.

"He is, but usually he keeps his mouth shut. Although, he did get into trouble once over his opinion about the gay agenda he was spouting about a few months ago." James wiggles his pointer and middle fingers into quotation marks.

"The gay agenda?" I splutter in laughter. "And what is a twirk? Is that some kind of a newbie nickname?"

James groans. "Please don't ask."

"I want to know." I fold my arms across my chest and wait.

"He means twinks. Grant's an idiot."

"Yes, he is." I can't help laughing at the miswording.

"Tim, please come back inside. I promise I'll be professional. We are both here to do a job and take care of those poor defenceless animals. What do you say?" He extends a hand to shake.

Damn it. Why does he have to be so fucking cute?

As I stare down at his outreached hand, my rumination of James's good looks doesn't abate the years of hurt this man put me through. Uneasiness and doubt swirl in my gut with James's good intentions than Grant's homophobic diatribe.

Even with James blocking me from caustic Grant, one good deed doesn't wipe the slate clean.

Yet, I saw a quote from Oscar Wilde once. *'Always forgive your enemies; nothing annoys them so much.'*

"Fine. But don't think for one second while we're standing here with pleasantries between us that everything is under the bridge, because it isn't. I don't like you, James Cannon. We'll never be friends, got that?" The finality of my statement doesn't affect him one bit. But I'm not done yet. I need to get all the words out before something inside me bursts. I take a deep, slow breath to calm my nerves, which is quite difficult while standing under the Texas sunshine. "I made a commitment to volunteer, so I'll stay. And don't put me with cats. They don't like me." I finally take his hand and shake once before swiftly pulling away, ignoring the sudden tingles along my palm from the touch.

"For right now, I'm okay with that." James winks and saunters off.

"What the heck?" Cannon winked at me like all is good between us. It isn't. My eyes trail after him, thinking I want to kick his... hmm, his nice bubble butt—*Stop staring at his ass.*

I have to keep in mind that James is just another hurdle to jump over before my life falls back into place. It doesn't matter if I must acquaint myself with a new state, a new town, and new people, but now I have to volunteer my time with my high school bully who is hotter than sin and wants to be my friend now.

With a deep sigh and an eyeroll at James's back, I head back inside and do what I came here to do.

THREE

Sinking down into the couch, my mind is in a whirl of exhaustion and excitement. Believe it or not, Tim and I worked well today. Not a single word of disdain came out of his mouth about our tumultuous past. Though, I didn't give him any advantages to talk about our mangled history. I worked on cleaning the pens while he set up the food and water bowls for the weened puppies.

Don't get me wrong, I want to make it right with Tim. Except for, there's more to my truth of wanting to be friends with a guy I had a secret lusty crush on in high school. And after today, I definitely want more from the feisty man, who on one or more occasion made me smile today. I want to explore our non-existing friendship. Even in the thick of our verbal tussle in the parking lot, there was an instant connection between us. I know he felt the spark too, especially the second our hands touched.

I want to explore what I've always wondered about the beautiful man. I always knew Tim had a big heart, and he proved his generosity today as he played with the puppies, giving each one equal amounts of love and attention.

My French bulldog Stanley, jumps onto my lap, pulling me from my thoughts. He climbs up my chest to give me his welcome home licks and butt wagging attention. "You're my baby, aren't you, boy," I coo to him. He slides down and flips onto his back so I can give him a belly rub he loves.

Stanley has been the only constant in my life for two years, when I adopted him from the very shelter I volunteer at. Seriously, there hasn't been anyone serious—not since the day I was forced to face the truth of my sexuality. Don't get me wrong, I had hook-ups. The Grindr app works well on my phone, but those were shallow one offs and sexual gratification only goes so far. I crave more than getting off. I want someone to share my life with—no matter how boring or exciting it can be.

Seeing Tim today—spending time with him—even in his silent presence, I wanted to confess to him everything that happened to me after graduation.

Cuddling Stanley close to me, I let my

mind wander back to the days I secretly lusted after Tim in high school. Secret was the total objective back then. If anyone from my town, my friends, or my family had found out about my feelings for Tim, the consequences would have been horrific. I would have been ostracized by everyone I knew. So, I did and said everything I could to get Tim out of my head. It didn't mean at night, I jacked off at the thoughts of Tim naked.

In the end, it didn't matter. I hurt him, and myself for being a coward. I don't want to play back the memory of how by my brother walked into my dorm room Freshman year and caught me kissing my boyfriend, and immediately told my conservative parents. Every hateful word was slurred at me by my father. And the final betrayal of my parents brought down on me springs forth from my mind, the attempt of conversion therapy.

Stanley nestles close to me, giving me his warmth and love. He's the only one who knows every facet of my life, and the hell I went through before I broke away from that physical and mental torture.

I know I have no right to think of Tim in any way, especially since he clearly can't stand to be around me today. He has every right to feel angry and hold hatred toward me. Hands down, I put him through hell, just to refuse to acknowledge that I was gay and was attracted to him. But fear was a great motivator for an athletic popular kid like me.

That was seven years ago. I haven't spoken to my parents or my brother since that day I called the cops, and I was set free from that life.

I still communicate with my younger two sisters, Lavender and Rose, who are as liberal as one can get. But they're back in California living their best lives, while I'm here in San Antonio. Alone.

Well, not so alone. I smile down at Stanley as he twists back to his feet and whines up at me like he knows where my head's at. "I know, buddy."

He licks my hand and yips.

"Want to go for a walk, boy? I sure need one today."

Stanley jumps off my lap, runs to the front door and yaps while his tailless butt is bopping back and forth.

"Okay, okay, I'm coming." I grab Stanley's body harness off the hook, but before opening the front door, my doorbell rings. "Hold on, buddy." I pick Stanley up and cradle him in my arms so he doesn't run out.

The second I open the door; an uncontrollable hiss immediately leaves my mouth.

It's Josephine Hennessy, Josie for short, my former boss and stalker. If not for her stalkerish ways, she'd be an attractive woman.

With short dark blonde hair, olive skin and big blue eyes, some men would find her pretty. I don't.

"Hey," she says, as her greedy blue eyes rove over my body. I quit my last job five months ago because of her constant sexual comments and physical attentions that bordered on harassment. She consistently asked me out, which I turned down. She left notes on my desk with hearts drawn around it, which I threw away. She went as far as disrupting my sessions with clients so she could watch me work, and that final straw was what broke me. I reported her to the upper management, but there was no proof of her harassment. Bottom line, she wouldn't take no for an answer, so I quit before the situation with her became worse.

The woman is relentless though and is aiming to make my life miserable. As proof with her standing on my front stoop and licking her lips as though I'm prime beef she wants to chew on.

"Josie, what are you doing here?" I can't hide the irritation from my voice.

"I was in the neighborhood and wanted to drop by and say hi." Josie takes a step toward me, a hand reaches out and snags the bottom of my shirt, as if she has every right to. Stanley starts growling loudly in my arms. She quickly drops her hand and shuffles back a few steps, adding a full two feet between her and my equally irritated dog.

"Good boy," I whisper to him, giving Stanley a scratch behind his ears. "Josie, I'm about to leave, what do you want?"

I guess my frustration isn't getting through to her thick head. "I… I miss having you around work, James. It's been five months, but now that we don't work together, I thought maybe—"

"No," I cut her off the second I knew where she's heading. "I told you how many times, Josie, I'm gay. I like men. I prefer dick. Period. Now I'm sorry if you think we had something, but we didn't. Never did, and never will."

To my utter shock, I see Tim—of all people—saunters up with a plastered-on smile and sidles up beside me. "Hey, baby." He leans up and kisses my cheek. "Sorry I was running late, but the traffic is horrendous at this time of the day," he says, camping it up with whish of his hand. He takes Stanley out of my arms without a single growl or bark from my dog. "Who's this?" He studies Josie up and down.

"Who are you?" Josie spits back like cobra's venom, while a scowl mars her face. "I thought you weren't seeing anyone. I would know."

How would she know? Has she been watching me? But I don't ask or want to know.

"I'm Tim, James's boyfriend and the absolute love of his life. And you are?" Tim's surly response is amped up, which hikes up my lips into a wide smile.

"I'm his boss," Josie angrily growls. Her eyes narrow to two pinpricks like two honed daggers.

"No, you're not," I flat-out say.

"Is that right?" Tim turns to me and winks, a signal to follow along. But that wink and Tim's sensual smile gives me a rush of want that goes straight to my groin. He turns back to Josie and says, "If my honey-bear says he doesn't work for you anymore then he doesn't work for you. Now, why are you here?" Tim leans into my body and a scent of oranges fills my senses. I automatically wrap my arm around him and absorb the sinewy strength of his form, his smell, and the way he melds against me sends another ripple of hunger through my blood.

"I don't work for you anymore. Please leave." I tighten my arm around Tim, while staring into those angry eyes of Josie.

Wanting her to leave, I turn my attention on the man in my arms and gaze into blue eyes that captured me in my sophomore year of high school. My attention lowers to his pink, full pouty lips and the sudden need to taste his mouth has me leaning down and stealing a kiss.

That simple sweet contact shoots adrenalin through my veins, jolting me alive. I thought I lived before, but now—against Tim, the small sampling of his lips on mine and his smell—I can see what's missing from my life.

Tim's blue eyes go wide with shock, but he hides his surprise from Josie.

A loud hiss from the woman has me straightening to my full six-feet-two height and turning to her. "I think it's best that you leave and don't bother to come back here, or I will have to call the police and file a restraining order against you."

"I can't believe this—What was I thinking of putting all of my efforts into changing you?" Josie storms away from us. "Go to hell, James. Go. To. Hell."

As I watch Josie get in her car, I feel Tim's body immediately stiffen against me.

"You can let go of me now," Tim orders coldly.

But I don't—not right away. His body feels too damn good. He fits so perfectly to me, like he belongs by my side.

"Sorry." My arms finally drop to my sides. I stare at Tim with my dog in his arms. Stanley is licking his face like he's the best treat, and I instantly get jealous over the canine taking full advantage. "This is Stanley." I scratch the top of his head.

"He's a cutie." Tim gives him a kiss on his face. "Now, why can't all dogs be like you? You're a cutie-patootie," Tim coos, and then hands Stanley back to me.

While my dog is trying to wiggle out of my hold, Tim gives him an ear scratch and then says, "See ya." He then literally runs away from us.

"Wait!" What just happened? I want to tell him thank you, or at least invite him in to talk. But Tim takes off into a full run the second he passes my ewe bushes.

I look down at Stanley, who stares after Tim and begins to whine.

"Me too, buddy. Me too." I strap the body harness on Stanley to take the walk we both absolutely need. Stanley to relieve himself, and me to mull over what just happened.

FOUR

TIM

I don't look over my shoulder as I hear James calling out my name. I charge around the corner of the block he lives on while my heart is pounding out of my chest. I'm not sure if it's from running away like an idiot in this late afternoon heat, or from the small chaste kiss James planted me with. Maybe both. Either way, I feel lightheaded and slightly dizzy, punch drunk off that kiss.

How fucking ironic that Freda lives little more than a block the other way from James's place. What's even more strange is me needing some fresh hot air after the day I had and I came upon James and this woman arguing. She looked like she was trying her damnedest to play the coy, shy girl next door, but her tone and James's posture told a whole different story.

I heard only bits and pieces of their

conversation. But my attention automatically fixed on the word gay.

Is James really gay? That can't be possible. I would have known... or maybe not—but that's beside the point. That bit of information is throwing me for a loop. I don't know if it's a lie, but that kiss proved unequivocally that James was definitely not interested in that woman.

I try to shake off that kiss, but his physical affection has short circuited something in my brain. A shiver runs along my spine as I slow my pace to an easy gait. It doesn't help the ache in my groin won't ease back. I can only imagine what I look like as I cast a glance down to my protruding shorts while trying to think of not-so nice things. But nothing's working. My dick won't take the hint.

Focus, damn it. You're supposed to hate that man.

But that simple kiss.

Yeah right. I might want to hate him, but I want more. More of his mouth. More of his arm tightening around my waist. More of his body pressing into mine like he owns me.

What if?

I shake that unthinkable idea out of my head. I should have never stopped and helped him. Nonetheless, I did tell James I'm a different person. Stronger. I'm far from that teenage kid pining for a jock that was too pretty for his own good, but is rotten to the core. But, I'm also a forgiving person. Maybe.

Forgoing the rest of the run—since I raced about a block for my getaway—I head back to Freda's place. Once home and alone, I jump into a cold shower to rid my body of the layer of sweat underneath my clothes and in my hair. While the heavy need is still evident between my legs, frustration runs through my veins.

The icy water should do the trick to alleviate my straining dick. Nope, the cold water isn't doing a damn bit of good. So, I chose to ignore my erection, get out the body wash slash shampoo and quickly clean up. But the damn thing is jutting out loud and proud, and aching for my hand. It won't be ignored.

My hand automatically slides down my soapy chest, my fingers wrap around my length, and I give a single pump before I hear Freda frantically knocking on the bathroom door. "Tim, are you okay?"

Shit. Thank Christ, I barely started jacking off. I'd be pissed off more at my friend for denying me an orgasm too.

"I'll be out in a minute," I holler past the plastic shower curtain.

"You know you left your shoes out where I accidently tripped on them coming into the house," she scolds, with another quick knock.

Not caring if I hurt her feelings, I call out, "Too bad. I had to go to the bathroom."

I rinse the body wash off me and get out of the shower. I snag an orange bath towel off the hook and wrap it around myself. When I open the door, Freda is leaning on the adjacent wall and stares at me like I have two heads.

"What?" I haughtily ask, stalking past her and into my room.

"Where the heck were you? I called several times, but you didn't pick up."

I pick up my cell and see all of the missed calls. "Sorry, I didn't bring my phone when I went for a run."

"A run? You're mad. It's ninety something degrees outside."

"Yes, I'm mad," I shout at her. "That's the whole point of running, Freda. But while we're on the subject of being mad, we need to have words about loyalty and truths."

"This is about James, isn't it?" she finally admits with a slight wince.

"Damn straight, I'm am… No pun attended," I gruffly add, looking right into her dark brown eyes. "How could you have done this to me? You could have warned me about James. You of all people know what I went through with that asshole."

Then why did you save his butt earlier?

Sometimes, I really want to strangle my

conscience for speaking up when it's not wanted.

"Because if I did, you wouldn't have volunteered." She frowns. "I seriously didn't think you'd be this pissed off."

"So-what, you did me a favor?"

"Tim—"

"No, Freda. You didn't want me there in the first place, remember?" I throw back the small argument we had, sounding like a petulant child. "But then you came back later, your attitude changed as though it was exciting news that I'd be volunteering. That's when you talked to James about me, wasn't it? That's when you two decided to concoct this plan to get me there so James to talk to me."

"I'm sorry. I was only looking out for you. At first, I thought it was a terrible idea for you to volunteer, since you weren't fond of animals, and with James also volunteering at the shelter. But when you mentioned you really wanted to, I hoped it to be true and you did move past all of the high school crap. I'd hope you to see James as the person he is now. Not the bully."

"I might have moved on somewhat, but that was my choice to make. My choice. Not yours, or his. And to come face-to-face with that man—well, I don't have words to express how fucking freaked seeing him after all these years," I let out a groan, and then fall back against my bed with exhaustion and embarrassment, feeling betrayed by my friend.

Freda sits next to me. "Maybe I should have told you about James. I am truly sorry for not explaining about James being involved. I didn't think you would listen. But Tim, James has changed. A lot as a matter-of-fact."

I don't want to listen to her thinly veiled excuse. Not until I'm calmer and I can think rationally. "Can I get dressed?"

"Fine." She lets out a resigned breath and strides out of the room.

I get up. "Thank you." And slam the door before she gets a chance for a rebuttal. Yes, I'm being a brat, but I have every right to be. Freda knew what I went through. The bullying, the name calling, and degradation that man had put me through.

However, she's right to admit that I wouldn't have listen to a word about James. And why should I? Not with the past we share.

As I drop onto the edge of the bed again, I closed my eyes and take in a deep calming breath. Maybe I should take up yoga? I hear it helps ease body tension... Or a bottle of tequila should do.

Now that my marbles are in order, I understand why Freda kept the news of James quiet. It has been years since I last seen the man. Although, she has to know he's still a trigger for me, even if she claims James, is a changed man.

My mind goes back to that kiss he laid on me earlier, and for a second, it felt real. Like we were together. *No. Don't go there, Tim.*

I quickly shake off the feels and get dressed in black shorts and a blue T-shirt from the LA Pride Parade circa 2018. I towel dry my hair—which by the way is desperately needing a trim—and head downstairs to face off with my friend again.

Freda's sitting in the kitchen, her head in her hands, staring down at the grey quartz countertop. "I'm sorry." The words come out in a strangled whisper. "I thought I was helping."

I let out a sigh before wrapping both arms around Freda and hug her tight. "I'm sorry too. I didn't mean to blast you with my anger. But you should have told me."

"I know. And you have every right to be mad. You were blindsided." Freda pulls out of my arms and faces me. "Please don't be angry. Forgive me?"

"Damn it, woman. Don't you ever do that again. All right?"

"Promise." She hugs me again.

"Forgiven." I genuinely mean it. I can't stay mad at her. Freda doesn't have a mean bone in her body. If she did tell me about

James, I would have dropped out of volunteering gig in a heartbeat.

"I need a drink. Margarita?" She wiggles her eyebrows, which has me chuckling. "With fresh mangos?"

"You know I can't pass up your fresh mango margs. How about you start the drinks and I'll warm up dinner? I think…" I go check the fridge. "We still have tons of carnitas and all the fixings left from last night dinner. Splitzies?"

"Oh, yeah." Freda pulls out the tequila bottle from the bottom cabinet.

After she sets up the blender, she cuts the limes, mangos, rims the glasses with salt and pours the tequila and blends everything together. All I do is warm up the dinner in the oven.

With one glass in me, I start telling Freda all about my day at the shelter, including the short run and the chance encounter with James, the woman, and that bone melting kiss.

Five drinks in, and a belly full of carnitas, I'm crawling into bed, blissed out with alcohol and a muddled mind. Or so I think as I lie there in the dark and my head conjures up James and his intoxicating lips.

If I wasn't so drunk, I would go back to the kitchen and down a shot or two of tequila to drown out his face and the insatiable need that's sizzling up from the depths of my alcohol-induced haze.

I don't want to think about James Cannon or how good his mouth felt against mine. I try to focus on all the bad things that happened back in high school. Especially, the one time, where he caught me alone in the locker room. Me in my underwear in mid-change, while he was full dressed and got really close to me like a hulking brute. I remember his words perfectly when I asked him what did I do to him to make him hate me so much.

"Because you're not worth it. I hate you so much for doing this to me."

As his words keep spinning in my mind, I unconsciously slide my hand down to my dick and slowly jack myself.

"What is wrong with me?" I whisper into the dark. How can I be turned on from that memory? It has to be the tequila.

With the lack of response from my subconscious, I keep on with steady stroke. I let out an audible groan, tighten my grip around my shaft and pump my hips until the familiar surge of electricity has me bucking into my fist fast. I cum so hard that I'm seeing stars.

"Jesus," I let out a muffled groan while smooshing my face into the pillow.

Once the alcohol-laden lust dissipates, something dawns on me about that day in the locker room. I didn't realize it back then because of fear coursing through my scrawny body, but it was there.

I remember it clearly now.

James had an erection. Hard and definitely big. He kept pushing his hips against me, but my focus was his hateful words.

Did I imagine that? Is my memory so eschewed by the alcohol that I can't remember it correctly? No. James did in fact had a boner. For me. That revelation has me slowly smiling.

I reach out, grab a bunch of tissues, and clean myself the best I can. Then I fell right to sleep with the thoughts of James Cannon and his big fat lie.

FIVE
JAMES

"What has you so nervous, James?" asks Brenda Ackerman, the head adoption counselor for this branch of the local Humane Society.

She is the one person I can talk to without getting judgments. Not that the other around us aren't nice, but Brenda understands me in ways most wouldn't. She, too, came from the same background of religious parents, and their rigid bigoted views on homosexuality. They aren't a part of Brenda and her wife Lee's life.

"I'm not nervous," I quickly blurt out, but my hands are sweating, and I keep wiping them down my jeans.

I scan the entrance way again, hoping to see Tim's smiling face. It's been a week since I last saw him, when he saved me from crazy Josie. I should have gone after him, but the smoke that trailed from his feet, he didn't want to talk to me. Not yet anyway. Therefore, I would give him the week before I approach.

A long torturous week. I seriously jacked off almost every night remembering how good he felt against me—and that kiss. I can go for some more of that. But I have a feeling, I'll never get a chance to kiss Tim again.

"Where did you go?" Brenda snaps her fingers in my face. "Hmm. Spill it, Cannon."

"It's nothing," I lie, but the look on her face shows she isn't buying it. I drop my head. "It's about a volunteer."

"What's going on? Do I need to get Cal or Trish involved?" Brenda insists. Calvin Bradley's the head of operations and Trish Yearling is head of staffing. They are two of three that do the firing and approvals of volunteers and staff. I swear Cal and Trish are a thing, but they are tight-lipped about it, and it's none of my business.

"No—it's not like that. Tim's…" My words drop off before Brenda picks up on who I'm talking about.

"Tim? You mean, Tim Scott?" The look on Brenda's face shifts from furrowed brows to a curious smirk. "You have a thing for him."

"W-what?" The heat of my cheeks spread to my neck, and I'm spluttering like a real idiot. I don't like talking about my love life at all, because it can turn into a big gossip. But I trust Brenda not to share it to everyone else at the shelter. "Umm… Yeah." I blow out a resigned breath.

"He's cute and single. I had a feeling about you two." Brenda shuffles the small stack of file folders of potential adopters. "I asked, you know." She bumps her hip to mine. Brenda might be in her late fifties, but sometimes she acts like she's in her twenties.

"What do you mean you asked? Who did you talk to?" I stare into her teal green eyes. She's a pretty woman, with silver hair and yoga-trained slim form. Brenda has been a mother figure to most of us and encouraged me to come out to the staff last year.

"I talked to Tim yesterday."

"What did you two talk about?"

"You know, this and that." She grins.

"No. Spell it out for me, please, Brenda," I urge quietly, leaning closer to her.

"Well, you know how I like to look over the new volunteers on their first day. I just so happened to watch you and Tim play the *glancing games*. So, I asked him how he felt about you."

My eyebrows shoot up to my hairline at her words. "What did he say?" I hate asking but the question blurts out of my mouth without thought. "Don't sugar coat it."

She chuckles, placing a hand on my shoulder and squeezes. "He told me that he dislikes you a little but is still getting to know you—but I told him how I saw the way you two were glancing at each other. All morning long. It's almost comical and sweet. Everyone saw it. He then blushed and walked away."

"Everyone saw us?" I inwardly wince at the imagery Brenda depicted. I drop into the seat next to me. "So, he still doesn't like me. Is that all he said?"

"Yes, but that boy can change his mind. Why don't you just ask him out? Let him get to know you." She wiggles her eyebrows at me. "Show him the real you."

"It's not that simple, Brenda," I admit with some reluctance, but since I don't have anyone to talk to about this, I let the truth out. Some of it, anyway. "Truth is, I went to high school with Tim, and with Freda, too."

"High school sweethearts? Lost love. Even better," she squeals with glee, both hands going to her heart.

"Shh—No." I grab her hands before she starts jumping up and down like a school girl. "I bullied him, Brenda." Those four words cut me too deep to admit, but it's worse when her eyes widen and a frown of disbelief appears on her face. Her reaction forms a football-size lump in my throat.

That knowledge of what I did as a stupid closeted kid will forever haunt me. Back then, my insecurity of losing my family and friends blinded me so much, that I didn't see what I had done to that boy. A boy I had a secret crush on. That boy who was openly gay and got flack for it, but had the balls stay true to himself. The same boy who's a beautiful, strong man now.

I envied Tim for his bravery—still do. I can't say that about myself. If my brother had never caught me in my dorm room, I don't think I'd be out today—not fully anyway. But I'm out, and here I am in a situation to make it up to Tim in any way possible.

Brenda tightens her hold on my hands and a stern, motherly look crosses her face. I don't think I'd ever saw her look at me that way. This cements me in place. "I didn't know you back then, James, but I bet you'll find a way to prove to Tim that you're a better man today. Show him your heart, and forgiveness and love will show you the way to happiness."

Her bolstered words are a reassurance, and an idea comes to me. I know what I need to do to make it right for Tim. I nod with understanding. "I will. Promise"

"Good. Because the way you two were looking at each other, I can light a match and the whole place can ignite into flames with how hot it was between you and him." She levels me with another honed look before releasing my hands and walking away. I'm left with a head full of ideas and a rising pulse at the possibility that Tim would want nothing to do with me by the end of this day. But I must try, for his sake and mine.

For the next several weeks, I'd make sure to pair up with Tim. Some of the women in the group won't like it since they have requested to volunteer with me. To staunch any of their ideas to date me, I'll make it known that I'm unavailable.

Then I put my plan in the motion, operation *Woo Tim Scott.*

I spot Tim walking in, and his smile lights up the entire entry way. A burst of nervousness shoots through me, but I quickly straighten my shirt and walk up to him and say hello. He eyes me up and down like I'm a crazed loon, says a hi and walks off.

At least he acknowledged me.

The moment he looks at the schedule, I know he's going to give me lip. But I'm ready to combat his anger with puppies. He can't be mad when he sees the new rescued French bulldogs with cleft palates that came in a few days ago.

I head straight there, prepping for what's about to come at me. And I'm right. Tim rushes into the room, eyes full of ire. But the second he sees what's in my hands, his anger crumbles in second like three-day old cookies left out.

"Oh my God—they are so adorable. What

are they?" Tim pulls the six-week-old Frenchie's out of my hands and cuddle them close.

"French bulldogs. Like my Stanley," I explain, with eager happiness. I can't wipe the smile off my face to see Tim melt for the merle and blue French bulldogs. My heart swells so much at the instant love he beams down at the puppies that small amount of jealousy ekes out. I wish he would look at me with such adoration.

Give him time.

All I have is time, but my heart is anxious and hints of fear of never be able to prove to this man that my feelings are genuine and true.

"I'll call you... Marble." Tim lifts the Merle, whose coat is a mix of black, grey, and white. "And you are..." he lifts the blue bulldog and studies the dog's face. "Your name is Slate. And you two will be mine. Want to come home with me, babies?" And then he drops down on the mat and begins to snuggle with them.

I leave a huge smile on my face as I do most of the clean-up, fill the water and food bowls and poop duty, all the while Tim is focused on the puppies. This routine was continuous for a whole month. Tim watched over the puppies while I tended to everything else. Brenda thinks I'm nuts, but I don't give a shit.

With each week, Tim talks to me more and more until there's no awkwardness between us and a genuine smile was aimed at me when he strides through those doors. And each time, my feelings for the beautiful man grows. I remember that boy from high school, but the grown-up Tim is funny, sweet, and smart. I love the way he laughs or give an easy smile for anyone. I even loved how big his heart broke for one of the puppies from a recent rescue from a puppy mill that died from Parvo. He cried in my arms. As sad as it was, I loved that he came to me.

Finally, it's time for my next step. Show Tim I want more than just a friendship. And I know what I'm about to do will shake the bridge of friendship between us. But I can't wait any longer. One way or another, I will have Tim in my life.

SIX

TIM

"You look terrible." Talking to Freda over facetime shows off the dark circle under my eyes.

"Thanks." I flip her the bird. She chuckles. "This is not funny. This entire week is dedicated to training and my head hasn't been in the game. My focus has solely been on James and how I made a total fool of myself for crying in his arms for a puppy that won't get the love it deserves."

"Everyone cries when we lose a puppy." Freda's assurance eases some of the tension in my chest. "But I'm glad he was there to make you feel better."

"Right—but I can' think about him, Freda. This past few crazy days between working my shift and finishing up training; today, I fell asleep at the table—surrounded by colleagues, while the head of nursing was explaining about new procedures being implemented next month. How fucking embarrassing. My head fell off my hand and cracked against the table."

"Poor baby," Freda snickers.

"Not poor baby—Freda, I almost lost my job. Anyway, I'm not going to last four hours of volunteering. I hope Martha has too many volunteers so she can send me home early," I admit with a yawn, while pulling into the parking spot of the animal shelter.

"If you're too exhausted, just let her know and go home," Freda says, with a munch.

"No. I want to spend some time with my boys. I haven't seen them for almost three days. They got their palettes surgery, so I need to see how they are doing. I'm sure they are missing me," I confess, whipping off my scrub shirt and pull on the purple volunteer shirt out of my backpack. There's more crackling noise in the background. "What are you eating?"

"Nothing," she says, this time with a mouthful.

"Spill, Chicca."

"Mmm… my Madre's homemade Chicharrons."

"You better have saved me some," I declare in a huff.

"There's a whole bag just for you." Another crunch into phone.

"God, I love your mamma's cooking." I

blow out a breath and slip the shirt over my head. "Okay, now I gotta to run. See you tonight."

"See ya." Freda hangs up with a crunch.

I shake my head, grab my bag, and get out of the car. Even though it's nearing eight in the morning, the heat of the day is kicking up and I can feel a sheen of perspiration across my brow. But my mind is on my boys.

I step into the main office and a blast of cool air hits my skin. "Nice."

"Hi, Tim," the manager calls out.

"Hey, Martha." I wave at her while making my way toward the back room where the lockers and bathrooms are.

"We have a new volunteer. Introduce yourself while you're back there. And please tell her the clothes she's wearing isn't appropriate for volunteering. What's she's wearing is for clubbing, not picking up dog poop." She points to the room.

I give the manager a nod, but wonder what this new person is wearing, that a sixty-year-old Martha would deem as club wear.

The instant I step inside the room and see a woman looking through an open locker that I know belongs to another volunteer, her clothing is the last thing I'm thinking about. "Excuse me, but people don't take kindly to other people snooping into their stuff."

She whirls around, and I stop dead in my

tracks the moment I recognize her. There, standing is none other than the crazy bitch that was at James's front door several weeks back. Josie.

Her mouth drops open, ready to say some sort of bullshit excuse when she realizes who I am. "You." I never heard a simple word come out more like an accusation.

I take an even breath, smile my widest toothy grin, and offer, "It's me."

"What are you doing here?" Josie spits out the question like its venom.

I drop my backpack and narrow my eyes at her. "What am I doing here? The question you should be asking yourself is what are *you* doing here—wait. I know why you're here." I fold my arms across my chest, and raise a high brow, waiting for a contradiction. She doesn't give it, so I go on. "Woman, you need to move on. James is into dick and from what I see, you don't have one. Or do you?" My eyes drop to the black spandexy-like dress and black heels. Martha's right about the clothes. And I'm correct to say, she was here for James.

She stomps over and points a red finger-nail at the door. "If you know what's good for you, you take your nasty self out of here and walk away from James. He was mine first. Always will be mine, and I won't give him up," she hisses, spital spraying out between her thin red-lined lips.

A rumble of laughter bubbles out of me, which eases some of the tension building my chest. I'm not afraid of this batshit crazy woman, but this is the last place I want to be in a cat fight over a guy. Especially, since coming off a double, got chewed out by the head nurse, I'm not sure I have the energy to deal with her.

But I look at her incredulously. "If my memory serves me correctly, you never dated. And I will reiterate since you choose to ignore what he told you the first time, James is gay. He likes men. So, if I were you, I'd take your scrawny ass and your half-attempt to convert my man and get out of here. And before you regret ever taking a step inside this place, I'll be watching. So don't come back." I stay firm. My hard eyes never leaving her raging ones.

Josie steps even closer, her four-inch stilettos raise her almost to my height. With our noses nearly touching, I want to step back, but I won't back down from this witch. James is mine. Besides, who in the hell wears heels to volunteer in an animal shelter.

"Are you threatening me, asshole?" she whispers.

"No, bitch. Not a threat, it's a promise," I say with a smile, which only seems to piss her off more.

One second, we're standing there face-to-face, then suddenly her hands are around my throat trying to choke me. Thank Christ for the few defence classes I took back in L.A., I'm able to knock her hands off me, but she tackles me to the ground.

I twist to get away from her and end up on top of her, and not a beat or two before, I'm hauled to my feet and a wide back is blocking my view. "Wait," falls from my mouth, before I realize who's standing in front of me. "James."

He looks over his shoulder, giving me one of his beautiful dimpled smiles. "Are you okay?"

"Yeah… But how?" But my question goes unanswered when James's attention is back on Josie, who is still lying on the floor.

"James, thank God you've arrived in time. That man assaulted me and threw me on the floor. He hurt my elbow," she whines while rubbing her arm.

"I did not attack you. You attacked me for saying the truth," I shout from around James.

"Yes, you did attack me, you—you forni-cator." Josie points to me like I'm the devil incarnate.

Really? Is that all she can come up with?

I bust out laughing at the absurdity of what she said, but quickly shut it down when

Martha storms inside and says, "I called the cops."

Eyes wide, Josie's cheeks turn pale. "That's not necessary." She picks up one of her shoes and then the other, before shouldering her purse. "I'll just leave."

"I don't think so, Josie." It's James that finally speaks up. "I told you to stay away from me. And here you are at the place where I volunteer, attacking my boyfriend. I won't stand for that."

Boyfriend? I like that he calls me that, but I keep that detail tucked tight to the vest. It's only wishful thinking to have James Cannon as my one and only. A friend, maybe. But an actual boyfriend? I shake my head at the absurd idea.

"But James," Josie cries. "I love you. And if you give us—"

"What don't you understand about me saying that I'm gay, Josie. I like men. I, like, dicks."

"You only need a good woman—"

"Get it in your thick head, I don't want you. I want this man." James curls his arm around me and pulls me into his side. "I want only this man." Then James leans down and takes my mouth in what anyone would call possessive. All mouth, tongue and teeth.

That kiss steals my breath and sanity away, leaving me blissful, but wanting more. James pulls back and turns to Josie. "There's nothing you can give me."

That truth must have finally makes her crack, because she drops her head and starts bawling. That's when the cops show up, and between myself, Martha and James's explanation, Josie gets hauled away.

While James is talking to one of the cops, I turn to Martha and ask, "If you don't need me, I like to say hello to my babies and head home. I did a double shift and I'm simply exhausted."

"Sure, honey," Martha says, before walking away.

Before James has any bright ideas and want to talk about that fabulous kiss, he laid on me, I rush back to the puppy area where Marble and Slate, and their siblings are snoozing. I give my boys a hug before rushing out of the building and head home.

Out of the corner of my eye, I spot James running out of the building. I knew he'd do that. But with lack of energy to fight off his charm—not to mention that mind blowing kiss, my defences are way down.

I really need to rethink if my days of volunteering are at an end. Though, I want to wait until I get the approval to adopt my boys.

Even so, with that kiss James planted on me, I know what I'll be doing in bed.

SEVEN
JAMES

As I watch Tim drive away, I get the feeling
this might be the last time I'll see him. Instead
of driving after him, I step back into the
shelter and head to the office, frustrated and
angry. The wild look in his eyes, the last thing
I want to do is jeopardize how far I came with
Tim and our friendship.

But I can't get what he said to Josie out of
my head. I'm his man. No matter if those
words were a lie, it came out to hinder her
from coming after me. Still, those words,
coming from his lips makes me melt.

Now more than ever, I want more. Especially, after that kiss, I'm absolutely sure Tim
is who I want in my life. But first, how do I
get the fear out of his head and get him to fully
trust me?

I drop down in the empty chair, curl my
fingers into my hair and tug.

"You're thinking too hard," Brenda announces, as she walks into the office and takes the chair opposite to me.

"Is the steam showing?" I counter with a smirk, popping my head up and stare at her.

"Pretty much," she says, tapping her temple. "Why are you here? I thought you were only here on the weekends."

"Normally I do. But I took a half a day off to run some errands and stop by to see what's on the agenda for this weekend and I... well, you know." I look away from her intrusive stare. "I'm sorry that happened. I never expected my stalker to follow me here."

Brenda quickly waves me off. "Don't worry about it. Martha had it all under control," she says with a chuckle. "That woman. You worked with her?"

"Yes. She was one of the three physical therapists I worked with at my last job. She's the same reason I left, and started working for Martha's husband's practice." I rub the back of my neck, feeling the adrenalin leave my body.

"I would have liked to seen Tim verbally kick her butt. However, I didn't want trouble for him or for you," Brenda says with earnest. "But the look on her face when you said you liked dick..." She covers her mouth and laughs.

I bark out a guffaw at her declaration.

"Trust me, Brenda, that woman needed to hear it."

"I'm sure she did, but what about you?"

I straighten in my seat. "What do you mean?"

"I mean, you have a wonderful man who defended you today. What are you going to do to show your affection for him?"

My affection. She's so right.

"I love him, Brenda."

"That's great," she chirps. "Then when are you going to tell him that you love him?"

Then a thought comes to me like a punch to the brain. "How about I show him instead?"

Brenda raises one brown eyebrow, waiting for my explanation. "I know the two Frenchie's Tim requested to adopt had their palette surgeries yesterday. Is there any way they would be good to hand over to Tim on Sunday?"

"I think they would be good by Sunday. What do you have in mind?"

So, I explain. About how Tim told me that I would have to prove it to him that I have changed. And since he's big into show than telling, I want to show him my grand gesture on how I feel about him. Brenda is beside herself.

Once I get the approval, I leave the shelter and call Freda as I'm on my way to work.

"Well, this is a nice surprise," Freda

squeals happily. "What can I do for you Mr. Cannon."

"Do you have it in your heart to help me set up a date with Tim?" Silence. "Freda?"

"What do I have to do—because I promised Tim that I won't keep any secrets from him," she says with a hint of worry.

"I promise you won't have to lie to him much," I rumble out a laugh.

"Much? Okay, you got me. Tell me what you have in mind."

So I do. Every detail of what I want to show Tim how much I changed and my growing feelings.

"Omg," she squeals into the phone. "I'm in —and I don't care if Tim gets mad. He'll get over it."

"I'm glad. Talk to you later," I say, feeling nervous flutters in my gut.

Finally, I pull up to work. I had fifteen minutes before my shift starts, I make one more call. Not even a full ring before one of my substitute parents, Moses Taylor picks up the phone. "It's about damn time, boy, you called." Moses's thick gruff voice rasps out in mock displeasure.

After my parents kicked me out of the house, I met Moses's husband, Mark Alvarez at a youth shelter, where he worked as a social worker. Since I was over the legal age, there was no need for adoption or parental consent, they took me and gave me the stability I needed.

"It's only been a week," I chuckle.

"Don't you know by now, we love to hear from you like all the time," he admonishes, with a huff.

"I promise to call more. But I have a favor. Is Mark near?"

"Ooh, this must be important. Hang on… Mark, honey, our boy is on the phone and wants to talk to you."

"I want to talk to both of you," I admit a little too loudly into the cell.

"What's all the fuss," Mark chimes in, with his usual bolstered Hispanic accent.

"I don't have time to fully explain, but I want to set up a date for this Sunday. Are you guys still on for the food truck festival?"

"Back up a sec, el cariño. Did you say a date?" Mark rushes to ask. "Is he cute? Do you have a picture? Text it to me. I want to make sure he's good enough for you."

"Baby, leave the boy alone. Let him be his own man. He will share when the time is right for him. Now, what do you need from us, James?" God, I love Moses so much. Believe it or not, he's the sense and stability in that household, where Mark is fun and full of life. Moses never intrudes, but both were and still are always there for me to lend an ear, a word, or a hand.

"Can you place aside a table and chairs in the shade for Tim and Me—and Mark, you both will get to meet him, okay?" I rush to say before he starts off on one of his tirades.

"Alright, but—"

"Babe, he has to get to work," Moses cuts Mark off by adding, "Text us what time Sunday. Talk to you soon." Then he hangs up.

I bust out laughing, knowing damn well Mark is going to be pissed for being cut off. But knowing Moses, he'd apologize in ways his husband won't forget.

EIGHT

TIM

I step into the shelter and immediately feel eyes on me. I do a quick scan around the space, but I don't see James. Though, I notice Brenda, the adoption counselor giving me a weird grin. I smile back before signing in and check where I'm working today.

If you guessed it, I'm in the puppy area. Again. I don't know who does the schedule, but I'm grateful they have me stationed there. Obviously, they must have heard I'm still squeamish about handling the adult dogs. A month of volunteering on the weekends won't make an animal whisperer out of me, so don't judge.

At least, I get to see my lovies, Marble and Slate.

Eyeing the volunteer board, I run a finger down until I see my name and who I'm working with. A smile splits my face knowing

I'm paired with Freda today. It's the first time since I started volunteering that we're working together.

Looking around, I'm almost glad my ex cheated on me. I wouldn't be in my happy place right now. I wouldn't be living with my best friend. Definitely not have met new friends, and hopefully, two dogs. And most definitely not have reconnect with James.

Heck, I'm more relaxed than ever since I started my new job over a month ago. Life is finally getting into the normal, and I like normal.

Which leaves me to one issue. How to handle the James situation? Most people who saw the fight between Josie and me knows my admission that James being my boyfriend is to be false, but the way everyone is looking at me, maybe I'm wrong.

Ugh. Why can't I get that kiss or that man out of my head?

No matter how much I want to keep hating the man, I can't. From his easy smile he has for me to the way we casually talk about nothing. I especially like the way he talks about his dog, Stanley, it makes me all gooey inside.

Even with all the past niceties these several weeks volunteering together, I can't have strong feelings for this man... can I? Maybe, if I let my guard down and clear the air between James and me, I can get rid of these wheedling emotions and move the fuck on. Once in for all, I want to—need to—move on with my new life.

Right now, I have duties to fulfil first. Two in particular. Slate and his brother, Marble. They came back this morning from the vets to get their palates checked. It's my job to take care of them and make sure they eat and drink without having any issues, especially since I see them as mine. I just hope my application for their adoption comes through sooner than later.

After cleaning the puppy pens, I set up the food and water. Then I focus on my boys. I sit down and stroke the little rascals' heads. With the dogs in my lap, I give them my full attention. It's almost therapeutic for me. They give me a sense of calm in my life, like they're only here for me.

The idea of someone else taking care of them brings a tightness to my chest every time I walk out that door, so I hope my application with Brenda to adopt them both goes through. Freda thinks I'm crazy to take on two dogs, but I don't care. I love them dearly. They're mine to cherish.

With Slate and Marble climbing slowly on and off my lap, I hear *his* voice behind me.

"Who do you have here?"

My heart practically jumps out of my chest

when James drops down next to me. "I didn't see you come in."

James strokes Slate's head and then Marble's. "I want to say thank you for sticking up for me on Wednesday. I'm sorry it turned physical."

"I can handle myself. But how are you doing?" I ask cautiously, while keeping my eyes fixed on Marble and Slate.

"I'm doing okay. Got the police report and I filed a restraining order."

"Good. Maybe this time, she'll stay away from you," I admit, this time meeting his eyes and surprise to see emotion in those amber depths.

"How are they doing?" James asks, as he leans in closer to me. I'm glad he changed the topic.

"The vet said they're doing good. They're drinking and eating just fine." I'm almost tongue tied as his thigh brushes against mine. I pick each puppy up and cuddle them to my face—a diversionary tactic, all the while thwarting off the energy James is giving off. I swallow at the trepidation swelling in me on how every time he moves, the friction seems to swell more between us. I put the puppies down and push forth to what I need to say to him. "James. I—I…"

"There's lots to say, Tim," he interrupts, but hesitates for a second or two before he continues. "But I don't think this is the right place to talk." He leans in more, his fingers brushing over mine while my hand is on my thigh. "I have to let you know, this past month since we've been working closely together, it gave me time to get to know you in ways I never thought I would. And I hope you got to know me more as who I am now."

I stare at him with bated breath, hoping for more truths, and I get it.

"I do see you," I say sheepishly, as heat creeps up my neck and pooling in my cheeks.

"I'm glad." His lips tip up into a radiant smile. "I have so much more to say—too much to say here—but I will leave you with this."

I tilt my head back slightly and look into James's amber eyes. I studiously hold myself still as he gets to his knees. I'm expecting more words but what I get is a kiss. Not like the one from before when I saved him from his ex-boss. No, this one is gentle and sweet, and I don't pull way. I savor his taste, relish his lips on my mouth, and the way his tongue strokes mine, its pure worship pulsing from James to me, and I melt like a stick of frozen butter on a blazing hot day.

Now, I'm not normally a melting kind of guy, but I never had a guy kiss me so beauti-fully that I feel cherished.

I gently pull back, taking in a breath—

absorbing James's scent into my lungs—and holding myself back from crawling into his arms.

"Since, neither of us is volunteering Sunday, please join me for lunch tomorrow. We'll talk about everything. Okay?" The pleading in his eyes has me nodding yes. It's all I can do for the moment, because my brain is in a haze of shock and need from his kiss. Needless to say, I want to stay in my small bubble of euphoric bliss and absorb the goodness of the morning.

Though a prick of self-doubt starts to stab me in the back of the head, popping my happy bubble. Instead of changing my mind to meet him, I shove those misgivings deep down in the bowels of darkness, knowing I might regret my decision, I finally say, "Tomorrow. But only talking and food. You won't be getting anymore kisses from me."

He nods in triumph, not sure what flashes across his eyes, but he leaves me with this. "Only food and talking." He offers up one of his victorious dimpled smiles before striding out of the area.

I don't know what just happened, but I don't get a second to think before Freda rushes up and hugs me tight. "Did I see James Cannon give you a kiss?" Her question comes out in a squeak.

"Did he?" Heat fuses my face even more

as I blankly stare after James and notice everyone is watching me. I put my hands on my cheeks and slowly turn away from their intrusive ogling. "I don't know, Freda."

"Honey, what's wrong?" Her worried tone cuts through my combobulated brain.

"He asked me out to lunch tomorrow," I utter, in whispered shock.

"Awesome. A date. You did say yes."

"Wait, this isn't a date. He wants to talk, and food is involved." I shake my head. I can't wrap my head around what he needs to say tomorrow when he can explain it to me now. And what's with that kiss? So blatant and out in the open for people to see—not at all what the old James would have done.

He's not the old James, you idiot.

"Tim, what did you say?" Freda's question pulls me out of my fog laden brain.

My shoulders slump while the puppies are climbing on and off my lap. "I said yes."

She lets out a squeal. "Now stop looking like someone kicked your puppy." She grins. "Seeing James isn't a bad thing."

I will soon see, tomorrow.

NINE

My hands are shaking as I stare down at the text from Tim. He waylaid my plans to pick him up, but that's okay. I'm still having lunch with him, and we're going to have that talk. This conversation has been a long time coming.

I text Tim the address where to meet. He's going to be shocked, since the museum grounds isn't the usual lunch place I would have set up for a date. But this isn't the normal situation.

No matter. What this is, is an apology on my part, and get-to-know-him even more. And hopefully after a belly full of good food and well-deserved conversation, it might turn into the date with the possibly of another sweet kiss at the end of the day. If not, then we walk away as friends. I would prefer the first.

Since there's no reply from the text I sent

to Tim, I jump into the shower. After I shave, I dress casually in a thin green polo and black cargo shorts. Staring at myself in the bathroom mirror, a string of doubt begins to strangle me.

I glance down at my cell to see if Tim responded, but there isn't another text bubble, which leaves me even more nervous. I hope Tim doesn't change his mind, since I know we both need this closure to move forward with our potential friendship and if I'm lucky, maybe explore what's been sparking between us.

I make sure Stanley gets some well needed attention. Several long belly rubs, and a quick walk down the block and back. Once I fill his water and food bowl, my confidence is waning thin with the ensuing silence of my phone.

This is all or nothing, Cannon.

In high school, I made terrible mistakes. With Tim, and with my life. He is the one person who still holds the keys to my past and possibly my future. I want to reconcile and prove to him how sorry I truly am for those years I tormented him. Some might think I'm doing this to get in Tim's pants, but my feelings are a fuck-ton more important to straighten what I broke all those years ago. More so than any sexual infatuation running through my veins.

I want to explore the innate connection I know we have with each other. I felt it in our first kiss on my porch, and the way we look at each other through these past several weeks. I know Tim senses it too. One way or another, Tim Scott will be in my life. He just has to give me a chance to prove it.

Tim

"I can't go. I'm too upset," I cry out. After finding out both Slate and Marble were adopted out this afternoon, all I did was mope around the townhouse with eyes full of tears. "They're supposed to be mine."

"Oh, honey. I'm so sorry." Freda drags me in for a hard hug.

"I don't understand it. Brenda told me yesterday there's a good chance I'd be awarded both dogs. What happened?" My heart is breaking at the loss of my two babies. Then James's text message breaks into my despair.

"You have to tell him either way. It's not fair to leave him in the lurch, Tim." Freda rubs my back. "You're not that kind of guy."

"I don't know." I suck back a heavy breath. I wipe the tears from my face and stare down at my screen. "I said I would go. But…"

"I think it's a good idea to cancel if you're not feeling it." Freda gently smiles and rubs a soothing hand on my back. "However, if you do go, James can take your mind off the dogs, and you might actually have a good time."

"I doubt it." But I slowly get ready. I dress in a dark blue tank, with a white open button collared short-sleeve shirt over it. I snag my favorite blue jeans that forms to my butt nicely and put them on. Thereafter, I fix my hair with some products, but not really having the heart to care what I look like. This is going to be as good as it gets.

I snatch Freda's car keys from the hook and say goodbye to her. I sync the address to the navigation James sent me. It takes me nearly thirty minutes to arrive at the location with a few minutes to spare.

When I pull into the parking lot, I'm surprised to see it's the Witt Museum. The small parking area is packed with people milling about. I'm lucky to snag a spot in the far row from the entrance off Broadway and quickly pull in.

As I'm ready to text James I'm here, I get a text to find him at the sign by the main building. Knowing there are several structures on the property, and the fact that I've never been here before, I use my walking navigation. This is the first for me.

Side-stepping people that seem to grow in numbers with each step closer to James, I quicken my pace until James is in full view, standing exactly where he said he would be. Something inside of me settles when our eyes meet and excitement begins to rise as his grin widens. I like the fact that his total attention is fixed on me.

I take the last few steps and say, "Hey."

But his smile faulters a bit. "What's wrong?"

"No-thing," I stutter out. "Why?"

"You look like you've been crying."

My heart trips over his words. I've been trying to rein in the heaviness in my heart for losing Marble and Slate, but my damn tears are ready to burst forth again. The ache in my chest burns too much, so I let out my anguish.

"I wasn't able to adopt Slate and Marble. They were picked up today by their new families." It's hard admitting my feelings and showing an ounce of sadness in front of this man. It's embarrassing. What if he uses my weak state and... I briefly close my eyes and shake off the negative thoughts.

If James was the same guy I knew back in school, I wouldn't be standing here in front of him. And, I wouldn't have let him kiss me yesterday, in front of volunteers and staff at the animal shelter.

"I'm sorry, James. I thought I got past the crying."

James draws me into his arms and holds on tight until my overwhelming feeling of loss for my puppies settle. He then whispers in my ear, "I have a confession."

I suck back a tiny sob and pull away from

his hold. I look into his warm, whiskey-colored eyes. "What?"

"Don't be mad, okay?"

I study his face a little more as I take a step back from him. "What did you do, James?"

"Trust me." He extends his hand in earnest. "Please."

I stare down at that hand in contemplation. Trust? The man who turned my high school years into a nightmare wants my blind trust? My stomach twist in knots, but something deep inside me shoves forward and utters, "Alright."

What is wrong with me?

Despite my fear, I take his hand and follow him inside the building. James leads me past a few dinosaur exhibits, through a throng of people looking at the encased enclosures of some animal habitats to a back door that leads behind the building.

"Where are you taking me, Cannon?" I try to let go of his hand, but he keeps a tight hold as we follow a trail that leads to a large parking lot with food trucks and a band playing on a stage. "What is..." and before I can finish my sentence, I see Freda sitting on a bench, with a big open box in her lap.

I glance at James, who has a sheepish look on his face. "Surprise." He lets go of my hand and steps close to me. "I wanted to wait until the end of our date, but Freda told me you got really upset with the news of your boys."

My heart started thrashing about in my chest at the anticipation of what's in that box. I look at Freda for confirmation. She nods, a huge smile plastered on her face. Without thinking twice, I rush to her. The sounds of cranky puppies yapping reaches my ears when I stop in front of her.

"Slate. Marble." I sweep my babies into my arms and hug them close to my face. They give me the proper licks of hello and I'm-so-glad-you're-here butt wiggles.

James sidles next to me and places a hand on my lower back. "I knew you wanted them both, so I talked to Brenda and she let me take them to give to you. I'm sorry my actions made you cry, but Freda thought you'd appreciate the surprise gifts," James confesses, as he scratches behind Slate's ears while my pup tries to bite my pinky.

"Do me a favor, next time don't listen to my best friend. I'd rather you be boring," I order, with another snuggle of my pups.

"Next time?" He kisses my temple. "I'll take that."

"Hey, I thought it was a good idea," Freda huffs, cutting off the protest of James's kissing me in public.

I aim a mock glare over to my best friend. "I appreciate it, but please keep your bright ideas to yourself." Then I turn to James. "As much as I like surprises, I thought we came here to talk and have some food," I say, my eyes on my lovies. My heart is full of joy, knowing another piece of my new life is set in place.

"Just say thank you, Freda." She laughs as she drops the empty box on the table, gives me a hug and takes my babies out of my arms. "I'll be a good auntie and watch these rascals." She put Marble and Slate in the box and strolls away with them.

"Hey, where are you going with my dogs?" I call out to her, but James takes my hand again and leads me to a table with two bench seats, which has a sign on it that reads, *reserved.* Thank God, the tall Oak tree is blocking a lot of the sun's heat or I'd be a sweating blob of yuck.

"They'll be fine. Freda says she'll puppysit while we eat and talk. Now take a seat, and I'll be right back." James takes off toward the nearest food truck that's serving BBQ. Hmm. My favorite food. It doesn't matter what type of protein they're serving, as long it's grilled or smoked.

Right then, my stomach rumbles loudly as James strolls up with paper plate full of BBQ chicken and a full slab of ribs. As I lean in to smell the savory goodness, a man, tall, dark chocolate in skin tone and beautiful, arrives with disposable bowls of coleslaw and grilled Mexican corn on the cob.

"Moses, I'd like you to meet Tim Scott. Tim, this is my good friend and family, Moses Taylor." James shoots me a warm smile.

Moses is completely bald, a body to envy, and is absolutely stunning when he flashes me his white smile. I also appreciate the ropy arms the man has as he leans over the table to shake my hand.

"Nice to meet you, Moses."

"It's very nice to finally meet you." He winks. "I hope you enjoy the food. My baby made it especially good today."

"What are you talking about, I always make it good," a Hispanic man says, who is just as beautiful as Moses. He pushes past him and extends a hand. "Hi there, I'm Mark Alvarez, the better half of this guy and the master of Grillin' Boys BBQ." He scrutinizes me for a second and says, "You are a cute one. James?"

"Yes, Mark?" James's eyes sparkle with mischief.

"I approve," Mark announces with a flourish and smiles down at me.

With the look on James's face, the approval by this man has to be significant, because James is beaming now. Or it could be the heat and sun at his back.

"Please, baby. It's enough of the bullshit.

How about, Master of the BBQ, you get back to grilling. We have people lining up to eat your food. Good to meet you, Tim. James, let's have a beer later next week?" With their parting goodbyes, James nods in agreement for next week's beer, then the men head back to their truck.

"They seem nice." But my eyes are back on the feast before us. "This smells so good, and I'm hungry."

"Me too. Dig in." James offers me several napkins before he grabs his plate and starts eating.

I enjoy the music from the band, the smells of the surrounding food trucks, all the while the tantalizing flavors of BBQ dance on my tongue. We eat like this is our last meal. Every once in a while, a groan escapes from James as he takes bites of the juicy chicken. Those moans have my stomach fluttering differently from hunger. But I quickly ignore him and eat the ribs on my plate, which are just as fall-off-the-bone delicious.

"So, how do you know them?" I ask, between bites.

James drops the chicken bone onto his paper plate and goes for a wet wipe. "Well, that a long story. However, since you're still eating, and I'm the instigator of this dinner, I want to start off by saying thank you for joining me."

"Thank you for getting Slate and Marble for me. Even though you made me cry." I mock glare, then laugh. "Seriously though, thank you."

"You are welcome." James grins, but hesitates for a beat or two before continuing. "I have a confession to make." He looks me dead in the eyes.

"Another confession? This must be serious." I drop the rib in my hand and straighten in my seat. "You have my full attention."

He drops his eyes to the table and rubs the back of his neck. "I had a crush on you in high school."

Did I just hear him correctly? "What did you say?"

"I had a hard crush on you in high school," he repeats slowly, but this time he meets my confused stare.

I want to shake my head and accuse him of lying, because there's no way what he said is true. Then remembering the locker room incident and James's hard on, I remain quiet and let him talk.

TEN

JAMES

Talk about nervous jitters. Here I am exposing my feeling to Tim as though I cut open my chest to show him my pounding heart. It helps that I'm shredding the wet wipes.

"Just come out with it, Cannon." Tim leans in and pull the wipes out of my hands.

"I wanted in your pants from the moment I saw you in freshmen orientation," I blurt out. No finesse or tact.

I'm an idiot.

A flash of hurt on Tim's face has my chest tightening with anxiety. The last thing I want is to make him angry. As much as I want to sleep with him, there's more than sex I'm seeking. Tim is everything I want in a partner. He's sexy, smart, compassionate, and so much more.

"Is that all I'm good for?" Irritation flashes

in his sharp blue eyes, and cuts through my rumination.

"No, Tim, I'm sorry—that's not what I mean—yes and no," I push, hoping he doesn't leave.

"Then what do you mean?"

"I was seriously into you back then, but that was a crush. Sitting in front of you now, I'm falling for you. You're sweet, and whenever you walk into a room, you light it up. You light me up." The second those words leave my lips, the dead weight of all the lies and secrets I've been carrying lifts off my shoulders.

His eyebrows hike up. "I don't know what to say."

"It's true. I had a major crush on you, but I was also jealous." I feel the heat of embarrassment and regret cresting the collar of my shirt and bloom across my face.

"Why?" Disbelief coating his word, but he continues. "I didn't do sports. I certainly wasn't in the popular crowd, and my friends were mostly girls."

I reach out, my fingers wrap around his. "Because you didn't care about anyone's opinion. You were gay—not loudly out and proud, but definitely out. You had courage to be yourself. That was something I couldn't do. There were so many times I wanted to tell you how I felt, but my fear got the better of me."

"How did you come out?" His eyes meet my gaze, while his fingers link tighter to mine.

"My younger brother. He showed up two months into my freshmen year and caught me kissing my roommate while we were jacking each other off."

"Oh shit. Like he just walked into your room? How did he handle it?"

"Not good. He left right away and called my parents. It was a terrible mess. My parents pulled me out of school, because they thought it was the college environment what caused my sudden gayness."

He lets out a soft huff of disgust. "I'm guessing that didn't go well."

"No, it didn't. But what was worse was when they brought me home, two big guys were at the house waiting for me." I release his hand and pick up a fry. I stare at it for a long moment, remembering the nightmare I went through for a month before I got myself out if there.

"They sent you to conversion camp?" The hitch in Tim's voice is mixed with tears.

"Baby," I say, coming around and sitting next to him. I wrap my arm around him and squeeze. "I'm good, so don't worry. I got out of there before real damage was done."

Briefly thinking back, I should have encouraged the guys and girls I befriended in that camp to come with me, but I was too much in a flight mode to think.

"What happened after you got out of there?" Tim asks with a steady voice, but he wipes a runaway tear.

"After I escaped, I ran to the cops. After they took down all the information about the camp and how they were treating us, an officer took me home. The moment I showed up at my parents' doorstep, they gave me an ultimatum. Either I pray the gay away and stay straight—their words, or I was no longer their child."

"I'm guessing you chose the latter."

"Yes. My parents disowned me right in front of the cops. My father gave me ten minutes to get my stuff and leave. So, I grabbed what I could and left," I confess solemnly.

"Did they get into trouble?" Tim leans into me, and I like having him close.

"Since I was a legal adult, the cops had no legs to stand on for child abuse or neglect on my parents' part. But the last time I checked, that camp was closed down and the pastor was in jail for child pornography."

"Where did you go?" Tim asks, wiping the wetness from his cheeks as he relaxes in my arms.

"My friends." I point to Mark, who's flipping chicken on the grill. "But I call them family. I ended up at a LGBTQA shelter, where I met Mark. He was one of the social workers at the time. He knew my circumstances and we became friends. Mark and Moses helped me get into a junior college and a job. They also gave me a room in their home to stay until I was able to finish school. They pretty much unofficially adopted me."

"What about your brother—and you have sisters, right?" Eyes still bright with tears, his warm smile gives me the support I need from him.

"John jumped on my parents' bandwagon and refused to talk to me until I got some help. To this day, I haven't spoken to him. But he sends me conversion therapy information online. However, my sisters are great. They support me and keep in touch on a weekly basis." Even after all this time, the pain of my families' rejection still hurts.

"I'm sorry you had to go through that," he says with earnest. "Damn it, Cannon, you're making a fucking mess out of me." Tim takes a napkin and blows his nose. After he sucks back a breath, a warm loving smile on Tim's face smooths all the hurt away.

"Let's dance." With our hands still linked, I stand and pull him up into my arms. I let the slow country music serenade us.

"Tim," I utter into his hair, which smells of citrus.

"Yes, James?" he quietly says, with a hint of humor in his tone.

"I don't want to let you go ever again." I pull away slightly to look into his beautiful, expressive blue eyes. "Maybe find it in your heart to forgive me for what I did and date me?"

A soft chuckle leaves his sensual lips. "I already forgave you, Mr. Cannon. But there's one thing I need to test out if we're compatible." He leans into me, his face inches from mine.

"And what would that be, Mr. Scott?" I move my head closer to his, wanting to taste those tantalizing lips again.

"I want a real kiss this time. No peck on the cheek, or a brief smack on the lips. An honest I'm-into-you kiss." I thought I did that yesterday at the shelter, but I'm up for the challenge.

"Challenge accepted." I close the gap between us, and kiss Tim like I always wanted to do. With my whole being. I want to taste every bit of his mouth—no—devour him with my lips and tongue and teeth. I want to show him, he's only one I want in my life.

Every inch of my body is set on fire from Tim's responsive moan as he melts into me.

I don't know how long we stand there dancing and kissing, but loud hoots and hollers from the crowd around us penetrates our passionate connection.

We slowly pull apart, our eyes never leaving each other. An understanding passes between us before Tim utters, "Yes."

"Are you sure?" I breathe in the excitement.

Tim nods, then breaks eye contact and hide his face against my chest. It's the sweetest look on his face yet.

A surge of excitement and jumpstarts my blood, and I whoop out, "He said yes."

ELEVEN

TIM

Embarrassment rushes through me when loud chorus of voices ring out from the nearby crowd.

"Take me out of here, James." I press tighter against him as he leads me away from the roaring group. With each step, the ruckus laughter quiets. I lift my plastered face from his chest and look around. "I feel redder than a tomato," I mutter under my breath.

"But what a cute tomato you'd make." The genuine smile across James's face melts my heart into a blob of goo. He pulls me closer as though he's about to kiss me again when I hear yaps.

"My babies." I spin out of his arms and two little bundles of goodness stumbles toward us with the speed of two drunks, tripping and tumbling over each other.

"They know their daddy," Freda chuckles

out, carrying the empty box with both hands. "They are going to be a handful."

"Come here, my babies." I scooped them up into my arms and they lavish me with kisses, while I squeeze them with puppy cuddles.

"They will be fine." James strokes the top of their heads, and finally looks at me, chuckling. He's so sweet that I can't ignore the growing warmth building in my chest, or my groin. "Can you live without them for one day and come home with me?"

Biting my lower lip, I nod without thought. "Let me tell Freda."

Right as I call out my friend's name, she approaches with a glint of a smile on her face. "I will keep them safe and protected with my life for the night."

"I expect no less," I say, then give each puppy a squeeze and a kiss on top of their heads. "Now be good for Auntie Freda."

"Dear lord," she mutters.

I give her a mock glare before putting Slate and Marble into the box. With a quick wave, Freda heads toward the parking lot. I turn into James arms. "Should I follow you?"

"Since you're not far from where I live, I figure you drop your car off at your place and we drive back to mine," James suggests, as we head toward the cars.

"Alright." I go pull away when James tugs

me back and kisses me with such ferocity, that I get lost in his taste, his lips, and the way his tongue strokes mine. "James—"

"I know, sweetheart," he grumbles against my mouth, before pulling away. "I will see you soon." He gives me a wink and hurries to his car.

I stand there, still muddle minded under James's kiss. I take a second and absorb the moment. Wow. I'm about to sleep with my tormentor from high school. A loud squeal escapes my mouth, surprising me and a couple walking past me. I'm feeling a major freak out happening.

"Sorry," I call out, before rushing to my car and climbing inside. I whip on the air conditioner because this is still Texas and it's damn hot out. I fumble to find my phone in my pocket and immediately dial Freda's number.

"Wow, that was fast."

"I'm freaking out." Jesus, my hands are shaking.

"Why?" Freda asks, as though she's just as freaked as I am. "What happened?"

"I'm about to sleep with James Cannon, my mortal enemy of all times." I shriek into the phone.

"O.M.G., will you calm your culo down." The cool reassurance in Freda's tone isn't helping my ease my nerves. "What brought this on? What did he say to get you so upset?"

"You left. He kissed me, and he wants to pick me up and take me to his place." After spilling out my thoughts, I realize what I said sounds stupid.

Granted, I've been holding a silent grudge for so long for what had happened in school, that I thought there was no amount of apologies in this world that will make me forgive him. Nonetheless, I want nothing more than to feel his mouth all over my body. I want him in me. Holy hell on a cracker. "I'm an idiot."

"No, you're not an idiot," Freda says evenly. "James was shitty back in high school. You have every right to feel unsure, especially since you only recently reconnected with him. But you also have to factor in that he's not that jerk from years ago. If I were you, I'd talk to him more about it before jumping into bed with him."

Freda's right. As much as I want to hop into the sack with James, something inside me is pulling the halt to our date.

"Yes, you're right. I'm going to talk to him."

"Good." She hangs up before I get another word in.

"Really?" I stare down at my cell phone before propping it up into the holder. I take a deep breath and put the car into drive.

My frantic heartbeats settle as I head down the street to where Freda and I live, but my mind keeps swirling around what I need to say to James. Although, my heart revs back up to hyper speed when I spot James's vehicle parked out front of the townhouse.

"Shit." My nervousness is making my skin feel tight. Seeing James and his great big smile has my body yearning for his touch. Damn the man for being too fucking gorgeous. Like Mom always says, "In for a pound." Whatever that means.

I turned off the car and get out, putting on a smile that I'm not feeling. James's smile drops off and takes four long strides to my side. "What's wrong?" He leans close and cups my face.

"James," I say, between a gulp of air.

"Tim." There's panic in my name. "What is it?"

"We need to talk." I look into his mesmerizing, amber eyes. "Please."

"Sure."

You have no idea how that one word gives me relief. I take another gulp of air before I explain. "I like you, very much, but something inside me is telling me to back off today. And to be honest, I'm still wrapping my mind around the fact that you were the guy that bullied me most of my high school life." I raise a hand and place it on his chest. "I know

—I know that's the past, and you're not that guy anymore. But I need some time to think, James. To process what we have is good. Can you give me that?"

I can see disappointment in his eyes, but in a flash it's gone. "I get that we have a fractured past, and I'm owning the fact that was all my fault. I'm sorry that I put you through hell, but I'm making a promise to you here and now that from this day forth I'll prove to you I'm truly genuine in my feelings for you. And, I'll be as patient for however long you need that time, Tim. As long as you know that I want you in my life, in my bed, by my side. Do you understand me, sweetheart?"

Sweetheart? Now I want to cry. No one—outside my mother ever called me that.

I nod to him, but he shakes his head. "I want the words, Tim."

"Yes. And thank you," I admit, with watery eyes.

He pulls me into his arms and hugs me tight. "How about we go play with the dogs for a bit, and then I take you on a proper dinner date."

I pull away slightly and look into his eyes. "I'd say today was pretty special for a first date deal."

"I can do better." Then he leans in and kisses me. Gentle and sweet.

TWELVE

TIM

It's been almost two months since that first date where he gifted me Marble and Slate, and the truth about his past. It took me a while to overcome my worries and trepidation that I sometimes felt when I was around him. James was a big part of my high school blithe, but with each day, he shows me he's the loving and caring man I come to fall in love with.

James is as good as his words. He gives me the space I need, and never asks about sleeping together. We talk all the time, and I like the direction our growing relationship is going. He never pushes me into anything more than kissing, and that's nice and respectful.

We hang out with his friends, especially with Mark and Moses, who are wonderful. They are a solid facet in James's life, which I'm grateful for.

Now I want to move forward with our

relationship. I want to be a part of James Cannon's life in every manner of being. I'm ready to express to James what I'm feeling.

With Freda's help, I set up a night James will never forget.

While Freda set up candles and roses, I cooked... Okay, maybe that's not the truth. I called Mark and Moses for their help. They brought over mash potatoes, gravy, and pot roast—which I found out, it's James's favorite. There's also green beans and homemade baked bread. All I have to do is warm everything up. Simple.

Then why am I so nervous.

To take my mind off, I go over the mental list and check mark all that is finished.

One: Got myself waxed. Cause you know this boy needs to have *it* smooth.

Two: Freda set up the candles and sprinkled red roses on my bed.

Three: Food is ready to be warmed.

Four: Take deep breaths.

"If you don't need me for anything, I'm going to take these little brats and head out," Freda says with a smirk.

"Thanks for everything." I hug my best friend.

"Just promise me that you won't freak out and you will have a great time. Okay? And don't worry about Marble and Slate. They'll have a good time with Auntie Freda." She gives me a kiss on the cheek, pick up the pups and heads out the door.

Glancing at the digital clock on the stove and realize I have one hour before James arrives. *Yikes*! I hop into the shower and wash myself from head to toe with the bodywash James like so much. I painstakingly pick the perfect outfit. My favorite pair of denim jeans that makes my butt look awesome, and a simple grey shirt that's easy to fling off. And let's not forget my hair.

After I take one final look in the mirror, I head downstairs. I light the candles and stick the plated meals in the warm oven. Right as I pop the cork on the wine, I hear a knock on the door.

"Right on time."

Not to look anxious, I take my time to the door and open it.

A whoosh of air escapes my mouth as I take in my man. Wow. James is gorgeous. He definitely knows how to make me drool. Dressed in dark blue jeans, black cowboy boots, he matched up a black blazer with a white polo shirt.

"Can I come in?" he asks, standing in the threshold with a bottle of wine.

"Umm—Yes— I'm sorry. I'm just blown away how handsome you are."

James leans in and kisses me sweetly.

"You're the beautiful one. Now come here and kiss me some more."

I do. I can truly stand there and kiss James forever, but the oven timer goes off. It's then James notices the candles and flowers. He's stunned for a moment or two, taking in the scene.

"What's going on, Tim?" But his big smile belies his question, and all my nervous energy is floods out of me.

I back away, head to the stove and turn off the timer. With two potholders, I take out the full plates and place them on the dining mats. As I pour the proper wine Moses instructed me to do, I say, "I want this night to be special. You have been so patient and under-standing for my feelings, that I want to show you just how much I appreciate you in my life. I care about you so much, James."

"I care about you, too, baby." James kisses me then he looks down at the plates. "Pot roast dinner?"

"I thought, why not ask Mark and Moses for some help with the food. I heard it's your favorite," I admit, feeling the blush fuse in my cheeks.

"What about dessert?" His smile widens and the gleam in his eyes becomes more wicked.

"That's a surprise for a little later. Dinner first." I hand him the glass of wine. "To us."

James tip his glass to mine. "To us and forever."

"To us and forever."

We talked as we ate, making plans for our future like we've been dating for years. But that's the truth of it. My feelings for James have grown so much in the last two months, it's like we have been together for years, and the idea doesn't scare me anymore.

After we finished the wonderful meal, James opens the bottle of wine he brought, while I grab two more glasses. Then I take his free hand and lead him upstairs to my room.

I flip on the light switch, and a warm glow from the lamp light filters through the sheer red material over the shade, giving the room a romantic mood.

I carefully place the glasses down on the nightstand and take the bottle of wine from James. The moment I place my cell phone into the docking station, music pours from the speaker, making the mood even more magical.

"How romantic." James's face splits into a lopsided smile.

"James." I pull him closer to me. "Dance with me."

Without a word, he wraps an arm around my waist, the other over my shoulder, and James hugs me close to him. Tucked under his chin, surrounded by his warmth, I feel so safe as we sway to Sam Smith's song, Stay with Me.

"You know we don't have to do anything but dance tonight." James is giving me an out, but I know what I want, and I want him.

I pull back and look deep into his whiskey-colored eyes. "I know, James. But it's been more than two months since we started seeing each other, and you have been so patient through all my crap."

"It's not crap, baby. I know you needed time to sort things out, and I'm giving it to you for as long as you need." He kisses my nose.

"And I appreciate it." I kiss James gently on his lips. "I don't want to wait anymore."

James's feet stop moving, both of his hands cup my face. "Are you sure?" Excitement coats those three words.

"Yes. I'm positive," I chuckle, feeling his eagerness against my abdomen.

He then kisses me. It starts off sweet, then turns into a hungry wanton need of mouths, hands, and now naked bodies.

I don't know how, but we end up on my bed, James on top of me and we're making out like two horny teenagers. In some sense we are—since we never got to do this in high school.

In the midst of moans and groans, our dicks align and James begins grinding against me.

"I want to taste you," I confess into his kisses, groping and grinding.

James pulls back and a salacious grin appears on his face. "I've been dying to taste you. Sixty-nine?"

"Sounds good to me." Without any argument, James sits up and spins around until his cock is hovering over my face. "Beautiful," I say in awe, with a single stroke of my hand along his veiny length. Not wanting to wait any longer, I lick the tip, tasting the precum, clean and man on my tongue. Taking another swipe with my tongue around the ridge of his head, James shivers, and that's my cue to take him fully into my mouth.

I work his flesh until he can't stand it any longer.

"Fuck, that feels so good, baby," James rasps out a groan. "I'm going to cum too fast if you keep doing that to me." He pulls away from me, turns and kisses me with ferocity.

"But I want you to," I whimper into his mouth.

Ignoring me, James trails his talented tongue down my body, and focuses all his attention on my erection.

I run my fingers through his silky short blond hair and grip it tight when he swallows me all the way to the back of his throat. I shut my protest down. "Holy-hell—that's… Oh —James."

His wonderous mouth has me nearly shooting down his throat, but James quickly pops off and orders, "Don't cum until I'm inside you, baby."

"I'm… Yes, please," I pant out. I point to the nightstand where I put a box of condoms and a bottle of lube.

James eyes it for a second and says with an easy smile, "You knew I was going to be a sure thing?"

"I only hoped you would," I reply with a smirk of my own. I have an overwhelming need to say *the words* to him, but something tells me this isn't the right time. Instead, I purr into his ears, "How do you want me."

He touches my cheek. "Just like this, so I can see your face as you call out my name while I'm fucking you deep and make you cum." His words send a wave of desire through my body, I shiver in reaction.

I kiss his palm. "You have no idea how long I've been wanting you."

"I think I have a good guess." James snags a condom packet and the bottle of lube. He leans down and ravages my mouth until he has me breathless. All the while, his fingers slowly and gently stretch me open.

"I need you inside me right fucking now, James." I keen out with pleasure, my back arches up for more contact with his body.

"Hang on, baby." He rips the condom foil

with his teeth and sheaths himself. Then carefully, James spreads my legs wider and pushes in a little at a time until he's fully rooted in my ass. Our eyes meet and a rush of emotions connect us in ways I never knew can happen between two people.

"Are you okay?" His whisper was so soft, I barely heard it.

I'm so overwhelmed with emotions that I can only nod. I grab the back of James's neck and bring him closer to take a long pull of his lips. Then I look into his stormy amber eyes and whisper, "Move."

James slowly pulls back and just before he slips completely out of me, he thrusts back in. He keeps with this rhythm until he hikes my legs up, my knees to my chest and starts pumping faster and harder into me.

"Fuck—Yes. Don't stop," I cry out in ecstasy, feeling the surge of electricity in my balls.

But James pulls out, taps my legs. "Get on your hands and knees." I quickly do his bidding and clamber on all fours.

Once I'm on my hands and knees, James pushes back into me. A collective groan echoes off the walls as he plunges in and out of me with quick strokes.

"Come here, baby." James hauls me back against his chest without breaking pace. His right arm wraps around me, shoulder to shoulder while his free hand grips my cock. He angles my head and tips his face in for a kiss.

The moment our lips touch, his grip tightens around my shaft and jacks me off in cadence with his thrusting hips. It's nearly too much sensation that I fall forward, bracing on both hands and ride the euphoric wave until I crash and splinter apart into bliss.

"James," I yell his name, as he shouts out mine, as we crest over the edge together.

We lay there in the aftermath of our pleasure, the quiet of the room with only the soft crooning of Lady Gaga serenading to us.

I slowly turn my head, and I can feel James's even breathing against my heated cheeks. His eyes are closed, but I know he's awake. Now, I don't know what made me say it, but I barely utter, "I love you."

James's eyes pop open, his amber eyes staring at me in great awe. There's a beat that I swear he's going to jump out of bed and run away. But he doesn't. Instead, he leans in and kisses me, long and thorough. Then he pulls back and says, "I love you, too."

I turn into his arms and snuggle in deep. I don't know where our relationship will head, but I hope it leads to forever.

EPILOGUE

Tim

As we hide behind several bushes for my friend Luke to ask his boyfriend Max to marry him, my anticipation for the engagement stirs my own want for commitment with James. It's been six years since we got together and every moment has been wonderful. Don't get me wrong; we have our rough patches here and there, but James and I believe in communication, talking things through and we never go to bed angry.

"What are you thinking of, sweetheart?" James whispers in my ear, then kisses the back of my neck.

"Stop. The last thing I want is to have a boner in front of our friends and their engagement party," I admonish, and pull away.

"Then tell me what's going on in that

pretty head of yours." James leans against my back, feeling the heat off his body. I love when he presses in close. I feel protected and safe in his arms.

"I'm thinking of us." I shrug. "Maybe someday we can get married."

"Maybe someday, who knows," James says with a slight hitch to his words.

I'm about to turn his way and ask what does he mean, when I hear Max and Luke walking past the bushes that a bunch of us are hiding behind. They're talking about something I can't hear, but my head is stuck on what James has said.

Maybe someday. I hope he means it.

Jarrod, Max's best friend and the owner of the summer house where Luke and Max had met, immediately shh's us. He then heads over to where all the family members and the rest of our friends are hiding nearby and tells them to be quiet.

Everyone has their attention fixed on the couple several feet away, waiting to hear the one word that will make Luke the happiest man alive.

"Yes," Max cries out.

That's our cue to rush out of our hiding place and surprise and congratulate the happy grooms-to-be. With hugs and kisses, and several bottles of champaign uncorked, we toast to Max and Luke.

I thought our day will end with a BBQ and maybe some hot and heavy sex with my man in the bushes, since it would be impossible to get intimate with all the family crammed in the lake house.

Then James surprises me by grabbing my hand and pulling me away from Max and Luke, who has a wide grin on his face. "What are you..." My words drop off as I stare at James, who is now down on one knee and has a small black box in his hand. My hands cover my mouth as his name comes out in muffled revelry of tears I yet to shed. "James."

"Timothy Andrew Henry Scott, I know we had a rough start in our friendship, but the moment you came back into my life six years ago and gave me not only your forgiveness, but your heart, I knew you were the man for me. You are my person, the one I want to grow old together and have children with. I can't imagine my life without you, sweetheart. Please say yes for our forever."

Tears cloud my vision as James's words wrap me up in love. I blink away the haze, and finally see all of our friends and their family surrounds us with baited breaths. I look down at James, his eyes pleading for me to answer.

"Yes." I frantically nod, and crash into my man for a bone crushing hug.

Everyone crowds around us, and yells out

in congratulatory cheers, tearful laughters and hugs.

"Just great. A double engagement," Jarrod announces, and tips back a bottle of champagne. He storms past us and stomps up the path to the lake house.

He's such a party pooper lately, but I ignore him.

Once I release James's hand, he opens the box and takes out the white gold band that has a row of inlayed diamonds in the center. His eyes meet mine and asks, "May I?"

I'm still too choked up to open my mouth and tell him hell yes. So, I just nod.

James gently slides the beautiful band on my left ring finger, kisses my hand and then pulls me close. "I'm so happy, baby."

"Me, too. I never been this happy in all my life."

"I think that deserves another kiss," James says with a wink.

I wrap my arms around his neck and look at my future husband and say, "Just one."

The End

A NOTE FROM CJ

Dear Reader,

Thanks so much for reading One Kiss, book 2 of A Chance At Love Series. I hope you enjoyed Tim and James's journey in finding the forgiveness, love and happiness in their lives. I had a great time writing their love story.

What's coming next in the series, is Jarrod and Miller's love story.

Speaking of love, please return some love, and leave a review on Amazon, Goodreads, and Bookbub. I would truly appreciate it.

Smooches,
CJ

ABOUT THE AUTHOR

Award Winning Author CJ Warrant can't exist without coffee, chocolate, and a damn story brewing in her head. She was born an overseas Army brat, in a Korean Italian household but settled in the states at the ripe old age of five. With a long career in the beauty industry, a wonderful marriage to a great man and three grown kids, her view of life is as such. Life is a journey; both good and bad, light and dark, but she takes it all in and learns from every experience life has to offer. She captures those crazy moments and brings her passion to life in words.

To learn more about CJ's upcoming books, giveaways, and events, you can sign up for her newsletter and be a part of her coven! Links are below.

www.cjwarrant.com/newsletter

www.cjwarrant.com

www.facebook.com/cjwarrantauthor

www.facebook.com/
groups/167874440806362

www.twitter.com/cjwarrant

www.instagram.com/cjwarrant/
www.pinterest.com/cjwarrant/
www.goodreads.com/cjwarrant/

ALSO BY CJ WARRANT

Landry Brothers Duet

Sweet Reunion

Sweet Redemption

A Chance at Love Series

Four Days

One Kiss

Dark Romantic Thrillers Single title

Forgetting Jane

Mirror Image

Dance of the Mourning Cloak

Coming in February
Third Book of A Chance at Love Series

Two of Hearts
by
CJ Warrant

1

Jarrod

"Harder, Mills," I moan, over my shoulder. Leaning closer the wall—ass out as far as I can stick it, so he can fuck me faster and deeper. Good God, I love how Dr. Miller Kane plays rough with me. Though, fucking in the storage closet at the hospital isn't conducive for either of us since we like to make noises, and that whole fraternizing rule.

Miller clamps his hand around my mouth and draws my back up to his front. "Keep it quiet," he says in my ears.

He pushes me forward, and start punching his hips against me. I take a hand and begin to stroke my dick in tight succession until every nerve ending in my body lights up.

"Oh, Mills," I muffle out, between clenched teeth. It's all I get out, before stars explode across my vision, and I'm a quivering mess and cum.

Miller clamps his fingers tight on my hips. With one final slam into me, he leans against my back and croons softly in my ear. "Fuck —baby."

Hell yes to that.

I don't get to absorb the full euphoric feeling we shared, before Miller pulls out, steps back and throws me a towel to clean myself up.

"Did you get my message?" I ask, turning to Miller and watch him zipping up his pants.

"Saw it, but haven't had time to read it. Why?" His dark blue eyes cut to me with a warning look.

"My friend Max and his fiancé is having a small gathering at their new house in Lincoln Park. If you're—"

"How many times do I have to tell you, Jarrod, we can't be seen together. One, hospital policy. And two, if Director Asshole finds out that I'm gay, I'll be out of the running as director. Got it?" The muscle in Miller's neck flexes with each word.

"Sorry I asked. It's been a year, and—"

"Sweetheart." He cups my cheeks with both hands, his words gentle this time. "Please, understand."

For a brief second, I want to push him away—tell him no, I don't understand. Yet, I do know the stress he's under in getting this position.

I let out a quick breath through my nose and lean into him. "I do."

"Good." Miller gives me a quick kiss on my lips and leaves.

Ignoring the pressure in my chest, I finish pulling up my pants and wipe away the single frustrated tear that Miller didn't see.

That's it. That's us in the nutshell.

Miller and I have been going at it like this for over a year. At the six-month mark, I was about to breaking it off with him, because I saw our hooking-up going nowhere. But then he brought up the subject about going bareback and thought things were about to change in our so-called relationship.

Bareback means, we get rid of the condoms and become exclusive. But that's all we do. No dates. No dinner and a movie. Or, nights out with friends who are also coupled.

I can't even describe the disappointment coursing through me.

I know eventually, I'm going to loathe this arrangement we have. I'm beginning to despise keeping us in the closet now—being Miller's dirty little secret.

I'm not a closeted person. Come to think of it, I don't think I've ever been in the closet. And I certainly don't want my relationship to be in it either.

Barring in mind, the pressures Miller's under so he can be appointed to the head director of cardiology is stupendous. And I know I have no choice but to keep our sexual relationship on the down low.

Except, I want more. I want what Max and Luke, and Tim and James have. I want love. I want commitment. Damn it, I want to have sex in my own fucking bed.

Stupid me, thinking it would be fun to get involved with a hot, older doctor. Until... I'm catching feelings for the bastard. Everything in me is shouting, to let him go. With every day, week and month that passes by, I'm more mindful what is lacking between us. But I keep hanging on. So, I keep ignoring my feelings for the man who set my body on fire with every single touch.

If I want to keep Miller in my life, I have to remain quiet about our connection in and out of the hospital environment. And maybe someday very soon, we can be out and proud with our relationship—I know it's wishful thinking, but a girl can dream.

In the meantime, storage closets and hotel room hook ups is what I look forward to.

I throw the towels in the bin, straighten my scrubs, and sneak out of the closet to do my rounds.

www.ingramcontent.com/pod-product-compliance
Lightning Source LLC
Chambersburg PA
CBHW051256170626
46809CB00004B/1672